MACHINE

A Green Moon Anthology

Compiled and Edited by

Matt Greenwell

and

L.N. Hunter

Foreword

Since the invention of the wheel, machines have been
an integral part of our lives.

Though ostensibly created to ease the burden on our
lives, these machines, more often than not, have taken
over, becoming an indispensable crutch to us.

Yet this is not the whole story.

We are at the mercy of more than mere physical
machines.

We are also prey to the machinery that drives our very
bodies and minds.

In Green Moon's second collection of short stories, our
authors delve into the world of machines to explore not
only the peculiar devices we have created to serve us,
nor even the contraptions that have us at their mercy,
but also machines as yet unborn.

The Safe Foundation are a Cardiff based charity who endeavour to help improve the lives of poor and disadvantaged people in the UK and abroad.

With a variety of projects in the UK, Asia, and Africa, The Safe Foundation extolls the virtues of cultural diversity and global inclusivity to foster a healthy community spirit in young and old alike.

100% of the proceeds of this book will be donated to this charity to help some of the most vulnerable people get access to education, health services, and those with other social issues reconnect with society in a positive way.

We thank you for your help.

Table of Contents

Panpipes to iPods

Eileen Holmes

It was hot. I squirmed as the sweat prickled my scalp and ran down my neck into my robe. The grit of the unmade road stuck to my damp feet and rasped at my skin. I sat on a low wall and took off one sandal at a time to clear them and sniffed at the stink. There was a green verge to the road, and I rubbed my feet into the cool grass trying to get the soft blades between my toes and sighing with pleasure. I lay for a while with my face resting in the grass, holding my beard away from my neck where it lay like a warm scarf.

The lane led downhill to the outskirts of the town. The buildings lay like a carpet over the floor of the valley. I could see a haze of fumes greying the blue of the sky over the tall buildings in the centre. Perhaps some of them would be my temples; perhaps the haze was the smoke of incense burned in worship. I was hopeful. This could be where I found my followers at last. This could be where I found music.

I drove the sun across the sky each day from dawn to dusk. Temples and obelisks were erected to my glory. Sacrifices were made to appease me, and precious herbs were burned to please me. I was the greatest of the gods under my father Zeus and the most beautiful. I was also the god of music and I needed to give music to Earth. It's so long ago that it seems like a dream. I went to Earth before dawn and the first mortal I saw was a handsome, barefoot boy tending sheep on a scrubby mountainside. I remained invisible and

1

watched him for a while, his rounded young limbs pleasing my eye for beauty. Then I was aware of the approach of dawn and put a suggestion into his primitive mind. He cut a reed and blew into it, smiling as it whistled like a bird. I left him playing with my gift and went away to fulfil my duty at the gates of day.

The street was now paved and stretched into the distance like a tunnel between rows of brick houses. With every step my feet slid on a film of sweat in my sandals. I tried to hurry down this brick canyon, but it stretched monotonously ahead, and I felt I was passing the same house over and over again. I was in the guise of a mortal but the few people I met stared at me in awe and hurried past, so I saw that they knew me. I tossed my hair and walked tall, flexing my shoulders, accepting their unspoken homage. It was many years since I had last appeared on Earth and I was gratified that I was recognised.

A group of boy children called out and followed me, laughing. I turned to speak to them, and they squealed with pleasure and ran to hide behind a wall. An older woman shouted to them and they retreated to a garden. My father Zeus spoke to me, his voice proud and strong in my head. "These mortals honour you, my son. Olympus is proud." I shouted a greeting to the children, and they crouched behind a hedge, continuing to call out and laugh. The young recognise my golden youth and long to interact with me but lack the courage to approach. They will become more daring as they age. I walked towards their hiding place to greet them, but they fled. It was, perhaps, early in their lives to meet with me. A small missile flew through the air towards me but fell short on the ground. They take any opportunity to touch me, these little ones. I laughed and walked on.

It was ironic that it was mortals who finally freed me from my duty in the skies. They discovered that the Earth turned round the Sun. I had no need to drive my fiery chariot across the heavens each day. I missed the adulation of my followers. Olympus became tedious, and I took mortal form and returned to Earth to see what had been done with music. I was amazed to find what mortals had accomplished with my simple gift. They now lived in great cities with temples erected for the worship of music – of me. Each temple had spires and towers reaching up to the heavens and a set of giant reeds making music for the faithful. The priests burned rare spices and wafted the smoke upwards to delight me. I returned to Olympus to inhale the adoration and the music.

At last the tunnel of houses came to an end. I must have walked here in the past, because a shabby brick building on the corner felt familiar. A small group of men sat on the steps of the building and appeared to grunt in recognition. A savoury smell of hot food teased my nose, and I felt saliva ooze under my tongue. I entered the welcoming open door. Ragged men sat at tables scooping food into their mouths. An old woman pushing a wire cart holding bulging plastic bags glared and shouted at me as I approached. Two women hurried to reassure her. They were obviously adherents of mine because they smiled and guided me to a private table. One maiden fetched me food and drink, a plate of stew with a piece of bread and a cup of hot tea. I ate hungrily, the gravy dripping into my beard as I soaked it up with the bread. I patted my belly beneath my robe

3

and pushed the dishes away to be removed. The two women approached my table and smiled. One spoke.

"Nice to see you again. How long have you been out? Have you found what you're looking for?"

I leaned back on the chair and smiled. At last, a mortal who knew of my quest.

"Ah – music. Where is music?" I asked. The younger woman took a wire from her ear and handed it to me. I accepted it graciously, of course, but peered at it with some bemusement.

"You put it to your ear – for the music." she said, and moved my hair aside, placing the end of the wire close to my ear. I looked about me with surprise. She had captured music in the wire, and it was sounding in my head. Mortals had obviously developed great ingenuity over the ages. I grasped the wire, but she took it and placed it in her ear. It was clearly precious to her. The food had been simple but tasty enough, and I thanked them for their service. I felt that I had not eaten for a long time and I wondered where the next meal would be provided for me. I must rely upon the mortals who know me. I rose to continue my journey, and the women looked anxiously at me.

"Be careful, Polly," the young one murmured, and I frowned at the familiarity. "Don't call him that. He doesn't like it," the older one scolded. "But she's right, you know," she murmured. "Be careful what you say to people. They don't always understand."

I accepted her concern. I'm far from Olympus here, and some do not know me. The spirit of my father, Zeus, spoke to me in my head. His voice resonated softly. "These women who serve you are your handmaidens on Earth. Take their homage with grace." I accepted his guidance and reached out my hands in farewell. The younger woman stepped back sharply in a respectful attitude, and I smiled at her.

As I lazed on Olympus, I learned that the mortals had sent great ships into the heavens in my name. I decided to make a visit to Earth to see what other honours they had done me. I came to find music. Surely it had reached even greater heights now.

I reached the centre of the city where people swarmed on the crowded pavements. They shrank from me in awe as I walked among them and turned their faces away. The few who were accompanied by young ones held them to their side and bent to whisper to them. They looked at me with wide eyes.

The buildings here had great windows which showed me my reflection before displays of colourful garments or small machines. I stared and gestured before my image, amused at the picture I made with my flowing robe beside the grey appearance of the mortals walking past. These were no theatres of music though, and so I turned aside from the wide boulevards. I needed to find the temples to see how music fared. The streets became meaner, the pavements narrower and many buildings had boarded-up windows. The dwellings were strung in rows without gardens, and the sound of barking dogs followed me. I hurried past these sounds. Dogs did not revere me as human mortals did. I have sometimes been pursued by snarling creatures with bared teeth.

As I progressed down the narrow road, I saw a group of young men lounging at the entrance to a yard. Fragrant smoke rose from them. I wondered if it was in my honour and so I decided to speak to them. They didn't answer when I asked them about the smoke, and I noticed that they wore wires to their ears like the young woman in the eating place. I approached one of the youths and tried to remove a wire so that I could join with him in the music. He slapped away my hand and snarled. The other youths gathered around me, and I tried to inhale the smoke they were making.

They laughed. My father murmured a warning into my head. I realised that the youths didn't know me, and I told them who I am. That amused them and they circled closer, laughing and blowing the smoke into my face. My father told me to prepare to defend myself, and my hand reached for the knife in my robe. The youth whose wire I had touched leaned close to me and shouted, his breath stinking into my face. I stepped backwards and tripped over an outstretched foot, landing on the ground. My knife slid from my hand, and the breath left my body with a painful gasp. They laughed and kicked me with their hard boots. I covered my face and curled my body and heard them jeer. The voice of my father was silent, and I felt his disapproval. I lay still. I heard them hawk their throats and spit. With a final kick to my sore ribs they left me lying on the ground.

I wept.

Where is music? Where is Olympus? Is it my time?

***

Jack and The Box

Beth Jones

Sarah closed the front door, resting her head on it as she did so. She exhaled and closed her eyes, tears rolling gently down her cheeks. After a few minutes she turned, gazing at her house. It looked cold, dark and unloved. Slowly, she slouched through the door to the lounge, and on into the kitchen beyond. She needed a brew. If there was one thing that could make things look better, it was a good cup of tea! That was what Old Jack used to say to her anyway, so she figured she would put his theory to the test. She filled the kettle and went to the fridge for milk. To her dismay, it was curdled and congealed in the see-through plastic bottle, and the fridge smelled like something had died in there. She sighed and rolled her eyes, and lumbered back towards the lounge, flicking the kettle off as she passed.

She sat on her comfy chair, the one Old Jack used to sit in when he came around for chats, pulling a crocheted blanket round her shoulders. She hadn't felt this alone in a long time. That feeling of being totally lost and unsure what to do; something she hadn't felt since her childhood. She sat for a while staring at nothing, thinking about Old Jack and what she would do with herself now he was gone. She'd been so busy caring for him for the last two years, she had almost forgotten how to do anything else. When he was taken into hospital, she'd been with him every day, trying to keep him in high spirits, trying desperately to keep him fighting on, but they both knew he was dying, and that it was only a matter of time. It was only a few hours since he'd passed, but the desperate need to see him again was like a black hole devouring her insides. He had told her not to worry, that everything was going to be okay and that he was happy to be going home. Happy that the pain would stop, for both of them. But her pain hadn't stopped, because now it was the pain of loss. The pain that takes away your breath and sears through your head, forcing every last tear that you own to come out all at once.

The last fifteen years, living next door to Old Jack, had been the happiest and most fulfilling she had ever experienced. She had no-one else in the world apart from him. She had been in the care system since she was eighteen months old. Both her parents had died of drug overdoses while she was asleep in her cot; apparently it was at least 24 hours later until the police found her. She was placed into care as her grandparents were alcoholics. She spent the next sixteen years being pushed from pillar to post, from care home to foster carer. She had blocked out most of those years; the emotional scars too deep to face. Throughout that time, no matter how hard it was, she had always been determined that she wouldn't let her horrible life define her. She tried hard in school and ended up a 'straight-A' student. She had won awards for her hard work in the face of adversity, and for her achievements in Maths and Science. She had always been fascinated by scientific discovery. Physics was magical for her; a playground of discovery where nothing was beyond the realms of possibility! When she was too old for the care system, she had been determined to make a go of her life as a fully blown, fully functioning adult. Social services had helped her locate a house – nothing special, a little two-up, two-down terraced home. That was when she met Old Jack, her next-door neighbour. From that day, those childhood scars had begun to heal. Now they felt wide open again.

Jack had been the closest thing she had ever got to a father figure. She managed a little smile as she remembered the first time she had met him. He had knocked on her door the day she moved in and given her a welcoming present of a jar of coffee, a pint of milk, and a bag of sugar. She had told him, quite bluntly, that she didn't like coffee! He had tutted and shuffled back to his door, then two minutes later had come back with a bottle of Navy Rum and two glasses! They had both sat on boxes and got acquainted over some very large measures. They instantly hit it off, as Jack had been a scientist all his life. She found him instantly fascinating, and pretty soon it had got to the point where they were always together, Jack sharing many wonderful stories with her, and her hanging on his every word, making tea in the gaps between stories, urging him to tell her more.

He had once told her how he'd been a codebreaker in the war. She had her reservations as to whether this was true; it felt like it was just one story too far, but by then she had so much love and respect for this wonderful human who had fallen into her life so unexpectedly, that she never questioned it.

Suddenly, a familiar sound came from the meter cupboard in the hall, and everything went dark. The sound was the electric meter shutting off because she was out of credit again. She swore under her breath. She really didn't need this now! She was too tired and numbed by the day to go out and get more, so she fumbled about on the mantlepiece for a lighter and lit the numerous candles she had dotted around the lounge for this very occurrence. The warm glow from all the little lights was somewhat comforting.

Then she saw it on the mantlepiece. The letter that Jack had given her when he knew he was beginning to fade. He had given her strict instructions not to open it until he was gone, and it had sat there, in the same spot, for nearly six months. She stared at it for what felt like hours, hoping that it would disappear. Wishing that she would never have to open it, but still more than a little intrigued by its contents. Jack literally told her everything, so what could this little envelope contain that she didn't already know?

Finally, she picked it off the mantlepiece and began to slowly open it, her hands shaking a little. Jack had the most amazingly precise handwriting she had ever seen; perfectly slanted cursive script, with every letter beautifully formed, and even when his health had started to fail, and he had grown weak, this skill never left him.

Dearest Sarah,

The fact you are reading this can only mean one thing. Don't be sad that I'm no longer here – I'm not in the least bit sad that I have gone. Nor am I worried about what is to come next. For me I should imagine it will be an extraordinary adventure!

I might be flying though space as you read this; or growing into a coral on a far-away planet, in a parallel universe, so have no fear for me. I am an explorer, and death is a mere diversion onto a new path!

I am also not worried about you, because you are strong, you are brave, and you are bright. More importantly, you are young. You have your whole life ahead of you, and you shouldn't dwell on my passing because to dwell is to waste time, and you will need all the time you can get to work on a project that I never finished, and have left just for you. I always dreamed I would have a daughter, and in you that dream was realised. I sometimes felt you thought more like me than I did, and this is why I am entrusting you with my unfinished work. I know you never believed my codebreaker story, but I want you to know that while my story was not entirely true, it did contain elements of the truth.

I was born and raised in Nevada. I did fight in the war for a very short time. I was an engineer in US military, until I was injured on manoeuvres and sent home. I took up a role within the military on my return, working alongside intelligence to identify and replicate advancements in our enemies' weapons. In 1957, I was working in the Nevada Dessert, at Groom Lake. You might know this place as Area 51. What I'm about to tell you, you must never tell another soul! You are the only person to know this about me. This is the reason I never married or had any children of my own. If I had done, I would have put them in danger.

In 1957, the ever-suspicious US air force were working on secret technology, to enable them to create indestructible and undetectable fighting machines, to ensure that there would never be another war that they couldn't win in the blink of an eye. They wanted to affirm their authority over the rest of the planet in a blaze of glory. The technology they were using there was not of this world. You've heard the Roswell stories: the conspiracies, the 'loony' UFO chaser tales. I can tell you now, they are all as real as the ground on which we stand, but the cover-ups have run so deeply that it is almost impossible to see things in plain sight now. As a scientist, I was enthralled and enlivened by the idea of discovering and replicating alien technology, but as a human being, with deep morals, I knew that this knowledge was ultimately destined to be used for greed and power, and I could not live with myself being a part of that. I spent months planning my escape; my own exile from that place. I worked through scenarios and theories endlessly before making my move. That is how I ended up here, in our little town, in the back of beyond, our little secret corner of Britain.

My point in telling you this, is I brought something with me. I managed to smuggle it out. I had found it while picking through some pieces of wreckage debris that had been shipped in from Roswell. It had been passed over by the other scientists as insignificant, so much so that it hadn't been recorded on any paperwork, so when I took it, the only person who really knew of its existence was me.

I don't know why it intrigued me so, but there was something about it that led me to think it was some kind of technology, some kind of machine not of this world. No bigger that a match box, and with no markings or obvious buttons, I often thought I might be reading too much into it and it was just what it looked – a lump of unknown matter. A chunk of stuff that wasn't man made or made out of an identifiable material. For years I puzzled over it. Right up until 15 years ago.

Right up until the point I met you. I decided pretty quickly this would be my legacy to you.

I want you to have it. I want you to crack the code. Unlock its secrets and come tell me when you have. I have no doubt that you will be more capable of this than I, and although I may have left this earth, this existence, and you will have no physical me to deliver your conclusion to, trust me when I say I will hear you.

Inside this envelope, you will find a small key. Take it into my house, and behind the fire in the lounge, you will find a small safe behind a wood panel. The object and my research papers are in there. They now belong to you. Carry on my work, Sarah. You now hold the key to the universe in your hand!

Until we meet again, Sarah.
Jack x

Sarah didn't really know what to do next. She kept looking up at the window, then back at the letter, suddenly feeling suspicious of everything. Was anyone watching? Had her house been bugged by some secret agency while she was at the hospital with Jack? Or was this just one of his crazy, mad science stories? She looked in the envelope and there was a small and dainty key nestled in the bottom corner. No, this couldn't possibly be real, this must be one of Jack's little musings to cheer her up, she thought. She looked up at the ceiling and cursed him under her breath. She placed the key on the mantelpiece and sat back down in the chair again. She drummed her fingers on the arm of the chair and fixed her stare on the key, which was glinting in the candlelight. After not too long at all, her curiosity got the better of her and she thumped her hands down assertively on the arms of the chair and pushed herself up. She grabbed the key and fumbled in her pocket for Jack's front door key. It was nearly midnight, and the rest of the sleepy road was tucked up in bed by now, even the curtain-twitchers would be snoring, so no-one would see her if she went round to Jack's for a little investigation, to see if her dear, crazy friend was just pulling her leg for one last time.

She opened her door, and stuck out her head, looking up and down the street, trying (but failing) not to appear too suspicious. There wasn't a soul about. Perfect. She tiptoed the few feet to Jack's front door and quickly let herself in. Although it was pitch dark, she didn't want to turn on the lights and raise any suspicion. Luckily, the clouds of earlier had cleared, and moonlight was streaming though the lounge window, illuminating the room with an ethereal glow. She padded silently to the fireplace. The house smelled of Jack. It was a comforting smell, like he was there with her, a protector on her new mission. She moved the old electric fire over and gently tapped on the 'wall' behind it. Definitely hollow! She suddenly realised that her heart was beating fast, and that all her senses were heightened. The super-power of adrenaline. She quickly surveyed the wall, looking for a way to dislodge the board. There, in the corner, was a tiny cut-out space, big enough for her finger to fit through! She slowly pushed her finger into the hole and felt something small, round and metallic. She pushed a little harder and, with a little pop, the whole panel moved and inch forward. She had to give it to Jack – a spring loaded secret panel behind a fire was pretty cool for a guy of his age. Slowly she took away the panel, and sure enough, there was the safe. She put the tiny key in the lock and turned. It was a little stiff. The mechanism was obviously old, but eventually it gave a little click, making her jump. Carefully, she opened the door, and there it was; a small, grey, metallic looking object, no bigger than a matchbox, sitting on top of a thesis of paperwork, all in the same beautiful cursive script that Jack had used to write his final letter. She sat back and stared, her eyes bulging. She had just opened Pandora's Box. Her head swam with ideas, emotions, theories, fears. She took a deep breath and reached in to the safe to remove the contents.

*

She got up at 6am the next morning. She hadn't really slept all night if she was honest. Way too much buzzing round her head for sleep. When she had got back in from Jack's, she had done what all scientists do; taken the 'Machine of Unknown Origin', as she was now calling it, to bed with her, put it under her pillow and had a good long puzzle over it instead of counting sheep. By 2am she was pacing her room reading the stack of theories that Jack had left with the MUO to try and find something he had missed. A few hours later, she lay back down. So many questions had occurred to her. What was it made of? Where had it come from? What had Jack seen in it that made it special? Hell, was this even a real thing or was this just Jack trying to give her a project to focus on, so she didn't miss him too much? If that was it, it wasn't working. The hole in her heart felt bigger today than yesterday. It felt gaping.

She slowly padded down the stairs to the kitchen and placed the MUO on the worktop by the sink. She flicked on the kettle and went to the fridge to get the milk, sleepily picking it out and holding it up to the light and realising that it was the same curdled mess that had greeted her last night. Angrily, she wrenched off the lid and went back to the sink to dispose of the putrid mess. Through her exhausted eyes, she attempted to aim for the plug hole, but missed completely, pouring the rotten stuff all over the work top, and covering the MUO in the foul concoction. She gasped and quickly bent down to get a cloth from the cupboard under the sink. "This is why I'm not a scientist," she shouted at herself as she knelt, rooting through the bottle of cleaning products. "The most important discovery in the world, ever, and I go and spill rotten milk on it."

As she fumbled, she became aware of the room becoming lighter. She slowly looked up around the room, her gaze finally settling on the light source. The MUO was glowing, from underneath, with a strange, blue-white glow. She stayed knelt down, frozen to the spot, her pulse audible in her ears. For what felt like an eternity, she remained there, transfixed at the enthralling light that was being emitted by this tiny object. Without warning the light faded to nothing. She slowly stood and leaned in closer to examine the MUO, her face now only inches from its surface. The spilt ex-milk seemed to have vanished into the MUO, almost as if it had absorbed it, but how could that happen? This was some sort of metal, she was sure of it, and it was smooth and non-porous. The silence within the room was electric, she hardly dared to breath. Time seemed to stand still around her, and nothing could break this fascinating moment.

Nothing would break this fascinating moment.
The MUO had her transfixed.
It had her complete attention.
But it did nothing…
Nothing…
Until...
…
CLICK…

***

Jack and the Box

The Woman Who Became a Machine

Kay Smith

Work was hard, but worth the effort. Cassie wanted everything done right. It made sense anyway, to plan lessons properly and produce beautiful resources as she'd been using them next year. Or so she thought. How was she to know there'd be a new Head of English who would change the syllabus?

The extra planning had to do be done at home, at the end of a busy day or on her precious weekends. "You can't keep this up!" Mike bellowed at her. "We've got no life. We never go out! You're either working or too tired." She accused him of being jealous of her recent promotion, and he had stormed off to the pub hissing "What the Hell has happened to you Cass?" over his shoulder. Her face burned. At least, she sighed, I can spend the whole evening writing reports and meet the deadline.

One afternoon, Cassie came in from work and ran up the stairs two at a time. She headed straight for the bathroom, pulling a pregnancy test from the depths of her bag, ripping it from its packaging. Then she spent the next hour curled up on the bathroom floor, numb with disbelief. They'd been careful, hadn't they? How could she have been so stupid? Mike would be triumphant. A baby would stop her concentrating all her time and effort on work. But a baby wasn't part of the plan until she had become an Assistant Head. She cried for two days before she told Mike. She woke in the night, sweating, finding it hard to breathe: would she still be taken seriously in work? How would her boss react? Could she cope with a baby?

Mike was ecstatic when she told him. All through her pregnancy he doted on her. When she arrived home, fit to drop, he put a cup of tea in her hand and sent her upstairs to rest. He cooked and cleaned, tiptoeing around so as not to wake her, while she secretly worked in bed, desperately trying to keep up, with the added task of planning lessons for when she had antenatal appointments. She marked until her vision blurred with hot salty tears. She let Mike believe her weepiness was down to pregnancy hormones. It was easier that way. How could she be the mother she dreamed of being, who read books at bedtime, walked for miles with the baby in a papoose or the pram, and prepared homemade baby food? She couldn't do that and be the teacher she wanted to be. She'd have to choose. That wasn't fair. It was hopeless.

When Lily arrived, a wonderful, perfect little diva, and Cassie fell helplessly in love. She threw herself into the long walks, savouring leisurely bath times, and freezing baby food in ice cube trays. But most of all, she spent quiet hours cuddling Lily as she slept, listening to her breathing and inhaling the intoxicating smell of her hair and skin.

"Why don't you give up work? Just until she's older?" Mike asked her carefully.

"Fuck you, Mike. How'd you like to give up your job?"

"You just look so happy, Cass. When you were working, you were exhausted. All the time. And nasty. We hardly spoke, and you never wanted sex. It's like you had double yellow lines wrapped all around you.

It's your choice, Cass. But you don't have to go back to how you were, working so hard all the time. You could take just a few years out, couldn't you?"

One look at Cassie's stony face gave him his answer.

He shrugged his shoulders abjectly. "I'm going to sleep in the spare room," he whispered.

Too soon, Cassie's maternity leave ended, and Mike's Mum came over every day to look after Lily. Cassie multitasked even more to keep up at work without losing any time with Lily, but it was never enough. She got up before 6:00am. She combined cleaning her teeth with having a shower. She had her hair cut short so it dried in the car, and she put makeup on at the traffic lights. In work, she ate at her desk while marking, at home she fed Lily while she marked, and got up even earlier to mark, mark, mark.

The crushing routine went on and on. Tough weeks became tough months, and then years.

On a rare coffee break in the staff room, Louise, a young teacher confided in Cassie that she was pregnant and overjoyed. "Maybe you could give me some tips," she added shyly. "On how to cope with being a working mum. You do it so well."

Cassie stood for a moment with her mouth open. "Are you mad? Why would anyone in their right mind do this job and have a family? Me, coping? Don't make me laugh! You can't cope with this job and a family. It's one of the other, or it will break you… It's tearing me apart." This admission stung Cassie like a slap. She felt sick and realised she had to go home.

As Cassie pulled onto the drive, Lily appeared in the open doorway, held back by Mike's mother. Lily waved frantically. "Mummy, Mummy, Mummy!" she cheered. This happened every day. Cassie sat silently in the car. She wasn't ready to be Mum yet. When Cassie finally went inside, Mike's mum made her a cup of tea, gave her hand a squeeze, then tactfully got her coat. The front door had hardly closed before the tears came. Cassie was weary to her bones. But she inhaled and became aware of the smell of a casserole simmering, polish and fresh laundry. Comforting childhood smells. It made her feel safe.

Lily, her ever so grown up 3-year-old, was watching her intently. She pulled Cassie to the living room. "Sit down Mummy. Up your feet on my stool. Don't cry." She dragged a doll's blanket from her toy box and then climbed onto Cassie's lap, and for several minutes tried to cover them both with the tiny blanket. Finally, she was satisfied.

Cassie felt herself unwinding just a little.

"Let's have a big cuddle, Mummy," Cassie managed a smile as Lily was starting to look worried.

Cassie held out her arms and said weakly; "I want twenty cuddles and a hundred kisses."

They lost count several times, and after a lot of giggling, eventually fell asleep cuddled together in the chair. That's where they were when the door slammed.

"Cassie? Cassie! Where are you? What's wrong? Mum told me to get home straight away. I…" Mike knelt beside the armchair.

"Shhh. She's sleeping. She's so lovely. Mike, I'm done. I'm not going back in tomorrow or maybe ever. There'll be other jobs, when the time is right."

Then, they were both crying and holding each other.

***

The Woman Who Became a Machine

MT Warlock

Louise Wilford

***Extract from the Public Enquiry into the case of
Edward Overdice, 9/5/2051, Orange County.***
*Verbatim recording of the statement of Gary Dowtreve,
CEO of Temple Transfers [gaps in transcript are where
Justice Thorpe asks questions]:*

"Yes, your honour, I was CEO of Temple Transfers for
five years, since its inception. I helped set it up – yes,
ma'am, with my partners Karen Schmidt and Munashe
Nkhata. I no longer work for them, no, ma'am – I left
last month… To take up a new post at another
company, ma'am."

*

"I agree, your honour, context is crucial. What you've
got to understand, ma'am, is that when the techsters at
NeuroTech Industries first invented Mind-Transfer
technology, it was greeted with excitement across the
world. Okay, okay, maybe a little dread too in certain
quarters, but *mostly* it was seen as a very positive step
forward. Let's face it, they'd been trying for long
enough, and people were losing faith in their ability to
continue to boost the economy. Their last major
breakthrough had been linking the minds of patients to
their artificial limbs so they could be controlled by a
thought, but that had been forty years earlier, several
lifetimes in Silicon Valley terms. Since then, they'd

25

been tinkering and perfecting and improving, but it wasn't until Marlon Tusk-Granville's invention of the MT Warlock that real advances were made. However, they're always up against the guys at BioMed, with their stem cell technology. It was a fight for the biggest share of the market. A fight for survival, really."

*

"The great thing about the Warlock was that it allowed mind-transfer to be used by non-scientists. You no longer needed a lab full of tech and a team of white-coated experts to transplant a person's mind into another receptacle. All you needed was the MT Warlock Mark 1 and a couple of headsets. Child's play. No, ma'am, I'm not saying children should have access to the sets. I'm just… Okay, I'll stick to the point. Apologies, your honour. Yes, at first there was what Dr Alison Cranston termed 'the Cyborg problem'. You see, ma'am, robot bodies were superior to human ones in terms of strength and dexterity, but no one had yet produced an android that could sense the world around it with the intensity of real skin. Obviously, developments in the world of genetics had created skin farms where human skin could be grown from stem cells to use as grafts for burns patients and the like, but they hadn't yet figured out how to keep this skin alive and fully functioning when draped over a robot body. The latest generation of androids still looked alien, and when they first used the Warlock to transfer minds to them, the results were disappointing. Oh, yes, the *mind-transfer* part worked okay. There's no denying that. But the minds that were transferred (the first was Marlon Tusk-Granville himself) reported a disturbing sensation of dislocation. They couldn't settle in their new home, as it were, it felt too foreign, too 'inhuman'. Marlon famously transferred back to his own ageing human body after only a week, claiming that he felt his original body – his 'meat suit' as the Silicon Valley dicks called it, begging your pardon, ma'am – was somehow *calling* to him. He later described his experience as being 'like accidentally wearing someone else's shoes but a thousand times worse.' I think it was something, some *problem*, about transferring a living mind to something that wasn't living."

*

"Okay, ma'am, I was just trying to give you some of the background, as requested. Anyway, Marlon decided the MT Warlock would work best when transferring one person's mind into another human body. I know, I know. There were nay-sayers right from the start, and the news feeds became hysterical, like they always do, calling Marlon 'Dr Frankenstein'. They have to sell the news somehow. And there were some religious nuts who claimed Marlon's work was against the word of God or some such primitive drivel. The usual suspects – you know how it goes with these things. But the thing is, Marlon Tusk-Granville was a *pioneer*, and pioneers are always misunderstood. And he was doing *good* in the world. Look, I knew the guy well – I'd been his PR man for two decades! He wasn't the raving loony monster the net made him out to be. He truly wanted to leave a legacy, to leave this shithole of a planet better than he found it. What's so wrong with that? Sorry, ma'am, I will try to moderate my language. It just infuriates me how Marlon is constantly misjudged.

Anyway, they started by transferring the minds of people who'd been paralysed in accidents – you know, people who'd lost limbs or needed organ transplants that stem-cells couldn't grow. BioMed are excellent at what they do, ma'am, but stem cells still aren't the answer to everything. Some bodies just reject lab-grown organs – some organs just can't be grown satisfactorily as yet. I'm no expert, but I know there are many folks out there in damaged bodies that can't be properly repaired, particularly if they don't have the money to pay for state-of-the-art treatment. Like those poor bast... Pardon my language, ma'am, I do apologise – those poor souls who were born into genetically-flawed bodies, ones that can't be fixed. Anyway, using MT Warlock, the minds of such tragic people were switched with the poor vacant minds of people who were in a Persistent Vegetative State. You know, more than comatose. What the docs call 'brain-dead'. This meant that, with a bit of physio and good nutrition, those poor souls with the damaged bodies could have a second chance at living with a *functioning* body."

*

"Well, ma'am, the brain-dead patients knew nothing about it, did they? They were relocated to the damaged bodies, but it wasn't as if they were *aware* of it. They just kept on sleeping or whatever it is they do. At first, they just used the bodies of PVS patients whose families had already agreed that their life support should be switched off. Before they died, their useless minds were switched with those of patients whose minds were fine but whose bodies were no good, and then the damaged body along with the damaged mind, died instead – it was essentially a whole body transplant. And people were okay with that. Many people consider that in such cases the mind has already died, leaving merely a useless body behind. But, you see, ma'am, there were more people needing bodies than people in PVS who were about to be switched off, so gradually – look, I don't know how it first started – pressure began to build to use the bodies of people whose families *hadn't* agreed to have life support removed. Yes, we can argue about the morality of mind-transfer 'til we're blue in the face, begging your pardon, ma'am, but the fact remains that it became legal. Yes, that's right, ma'am, the Enforced Body Donation Act of 2253. Yes, I know it was very controversial and it's certainly true that, after her accident, President Li was the most vociferous campaigner for the new law and one of the first people to take advantage of it… No, I'm not implying anything, your honour. I'm just stating the facts. The point is, ma'am, that this new law kind of opened up the market, you might say. People started trying to work out how else they could monetise the technology. And then Marlon died and left his research to the country, and that seemed to open up the floodgates. Everyone wanted a piece of the action. And *that* was when we got the boom in MT start-ups, including Temple Transfers. We were one of the first non-medi companies to make money out of the Warlock. It was a simple idea – Karen Schmidt came up with it first. Basically, there were lots of unfit, overweight people out there, ruining their health, costing the healthcare companies billions of dollars, and some of these people were very rich. Now, these people weren't going to get off their fat backsides, begging your pardon, ma'am, or they'd've already done it. Rich people prefer to buy their way out of their problems. They'd usually tried all the normal things people with money do to look and feel better – the surgical options, the personal chefs, etc. But they were still obese. They needed – well, Karen called it 'a personal trainer', someone who would swap minds with them for a set period of time and get their bodies trim and fit while they enjoyed the pleasures of the healthy, beautiful bodies of the personal trainers."

*

"Yes, ma'am, there *were* a large number of applicants for the jobs, weird as it sounds. We paid them very well indeed – much more than they could make any other way. They had to be young, fit and attractive, and they were all psyche-tested to ensure they had the right kind of personality. It takes real stamina to take over a weak, flabby, unfit unit – that's the jargon we use in the industry, ma'am: a unit just means a body – and train it to good health, enduring all the pain and self-deprivation that entails. But our trainers were used to self-discipline. It also takes a certain kind of person to be willing to let some fat slob take over their super-fit body for a few months in their absence. I tell you, ma'am, some of those poor trainers returned to find they'd put on fifty pounds and lost all their muscle tone, so they had to spend several months getting back in shape themselves. We provided state-of-the-art gyms and nutritional programmes, all the help we could, because we wanted them to go through it all again. Not everyone did, of course. Some of them set out just to do one tour of duty – that's what they call it, ma'am – but others worked for us for years. Of course, ma'am, there were one or two casualties. That was one reason for their huge salary. As you are aware, ma'am, employers can impose any conditions they want on their employees as long as the employee understands their contract and has agreed to it. Our Personal Trainers were elite employees, paid accordingly, and they agreed very willingly to the terms and conditions. It's the poor saps on minimum wage who have to take it or starve, and that's the real scandal of the world we live in. Hell, I'm a rich guy myself, but even I can see the inequities in the labour market. But, as I say, we rewarded our employees very well indeed and we therefore expected them to accept our rules. PT's were obliged to do everything they could to improve the health and well-being of the bodies they were inhabiting. The bodies of our rich clients belonged to the clients throughout the process – that was one of our main rules. The PT's were *borrowing* their clients' bodies temporarily and were expected to look after them as if they were their own. We had lots of rules for both parties – no drugs, limited alcohol, no life-threatening activities, that sort of thing. But, well, rich people don't always take kindly to rules – they often think the rules don't apply to them. We had several trainers who returned to their own bodies only to find they were addicted to heroin, or alcohol, or had serious injuries from stupid avoidable accidents, or sexually-transmitted diseases, begging your pardon, your honour. We had an agreement, written into the contact, that, in the event of the PT's original body being no longer available for them to return to – if it had *expired*, shall we say – then their minds would be transferred into the next available PVS patient. By that time, minds could be stored in Warlock's memory banks until a suitable vessel became available. It was a risk that a surprising number of people were prepared to take. Look, it's a harsh world out there, your honour – young people can't always find jobs very easily, and the ones they do find don't always pay well. Even college graduates struggle to make a living. Hell, we all know how tough it is outside the Valley. People saw themselves as exceptionally fortunate to get a job with us as a PT. It changed their lives. And the fact that many of them did more than one tour tells you that they enjoyed the work, thought it worthwhile. Hell, some of them became friends with the people they'd got fit, working as more conventional types of personal trainers for them. That happened quite a few times, though I must admit that most of those fat-ass billionaires just put on the weight again and had to call on our services multiple times. It's human nature, I'm afraid."

*

"Well, your honour, if the *client's* body dies with the PT *in situ*, as it were, our contracts state that the client retains possession of the PT's body. Yes, it is one rule for the client, another for the PT. You see, the clients pay us to store a back-up copy of their minds that we can transfer into the client's newly-fit body in the event that something happens to the client's mind while it is in the PT's body. It's a kind of insurance policy. It isn't perfect – there's a degree of memory loss, even some intellectual impairment in some cases, but it means that the clients will always leave Temple Transfers inside a healthy body. And it costs a fortune to back-up a mind, far more than our PT's could afford, which is why we don't keep copies of the minds of our PT's. We are prepared to store their minds if they find themselves without a body, until a PVS body can be found for them, but we don't store back-ups. However, the clients have the right to take full possession of the PT's body if the client's own body is destroyed or seriously damaged, whereas the PT's are always *only temporarily in charge* of the client's body. They are care-taking it, if you will. Renovating it. But it is never theirs. That's what they agree to when they sign our contracts. And, since most people have a powerful emotional link to their own bodies, it generally works out. There was only one previous occasion when a client's body had been destroyed – yes, ma'am, the Barnum-MacGregor case. Erica Barnum took over the body of Felicity MacGregor, after her own body (and sadly Felicity's mind) was irretrievably damaged in a fire. The case was the first of its kind to go through the courts and, as you know, ma'am, it made legal history. The Supreme Court ruled, by a narrow margin, that the body of Felicity MacGregor now *belonged* to Erica Barnum, so that in effect it *became* Erica Barnum. Hell, some people think it redefined what it means to be human. It certainly raised questions about the nature of identity, even I can see that. But I'm not an academic, ma'am, I'm a businessman. I don't have an opinion on such issues."

*

"Okay, ma'am, well, I'm getting there. When we employed him, Edward Overdice seemed to be a typical PT – late twenties, very fit, good-looking, intelligent, calm in a crisis, highly disciplined. He'd trained in the army, officer training, and done one tour of North Korea, but he'd left because he didn't feel he was getting anywhere. He was an ambitious type, wanted to start up his own company. He was doing PT work to get the money to do this, which seemed a laudable ambition. He passed all the psyche tests."

*

"Yes, I am aware of Dr Fillian's criticisms of the tests we used, but they are industry-standard tests. They've been used for years. He passed all the psychopathy tests and was cleared A-One. Then he went on and passed every other test we threw at him with flying colours. I mean, the guy was a *model* employee. I guess that alone makes him a little unusual, but we're used to high fliers at Temple Transfers. Walden Percival? Well, he was in many ways a typical fat-suit – sorry, your honour, that's what we called the clients, for shorthand. Not to their faces, no. Yes, I realise it does sound disrespectful. I'm sorry. I won't do it again, ma'am. Anyway, as I was saying, Walden was the only son of a billionaire VR magnate who'd recently inherited his father's money. He was the sole inheritor, too. His mother had died some years back. He had no siblings. Walden was 36-years-old, but he was so fat, he was more like a man in his fifties in terms of the condition of his heart and lungs, his other internal organs, his joints and bones and muscles. He weighed in at over 280 pounds! He wanted to marry Casey Lonnegan – you know, the actress? She'd given him an ultimatum that he must lose at least 56 pounds before she'd even consider him. Even his money didn't sway that girl, your honour. Shows a certain amount of character, I think, say what you like about her. So, anyway, Walden decided to use Temple Transfers. Now in such a case, we have special deals because of the surgery needed. When you're that fat, your honour, you lose the weight but you can be left carrying round pounds of spare skin, so you have to have it surgically removed. Our clients pay extra to have the PT's stay in their bodies until they've recovered from the surgery, and then they give their new slim bodies a few weeks of topping up to get them super-fit again before their original owner takes repossession, as it were. The PT's get an extra bonus for agreeing to this. Walden Percival was an extremely lucrative client, but he was what we call a Risk-Eight. That means, there was a high chance of him dying while the PT was in his body – the guy was obese, as I said, but he also had a whole raft of weight-related health problems. It was going to be a mammoth task to get his body in shape. And then there are always risks to surgery too. Edward Overdice agreed to the terms of the contract and he was paid a handsome fee, including his surgery bonus – half at the start of the contract and the rest to be paid at the end. Standard terms, your honour. The Mind-Transfer went ahead without a hitch. He reported some physical discomfort at first after he took over Walden Percival's body, but I don't believe it was as bad as he later reported. Sure, it must have been difficult at first for Overdice, getting that huge unfit body to start exercising, and reducing its calorie intake so drastically. But Overdice was a professional. He was determined that Walden Percival was going to be a different man by the time they swapped back. Gradually, the weight started coming off and the muscle tone improved. Overdice worked like a robot, your honour, and I am not being robotist when I say that. I mean, he worked day and night, week after week, ensuring that body ate the right foods, did the right exercise, got the right amount of sleep. By the time he'd finished, Walden Percival's body was half its original size and in peak condition except for the excess skin. Just before the operation, Casey Lonnegan came to visit him in hospital. No, your honour, it was very unusual. Clients and their associates are usually advised to stay well apart from PT's during the training, for psychological reasons. It can cause serious disorientation seeing your own body, or that of a close friend or family member, housing someone else's personality. It has been described as feeling like the person you love has been *possessed*, taken over. But there was no actual rule against it. Lonnegan said she wanted to tell Edward Overdice how grateful Walden was for what Edward was doing for him. I was there, your honour, along with several other Temple Transfer executives, and we all felt it was a moving encounter. Casey Lonnegan told Overdice that she was so impressed by Walden's improved physique that, assuming the operation went well, she'd agreed to marry Walden afterwards. She wanted to thank Overdice for all his hard work. But I must admit it was a little weird, your honour – I mean, Casey was speaking to the body belonging to the man she was going to marry, even though she was speaking to the mind of a virtual stranger. It was a peculiar scene, ma'am, but that's something you get used to working in the world of Mind-Transfer technology. Anyway, the operation went ahead as planned and everything ran like clockwork. Walden Percival's body woke up the next day with his excess skin removed. It would take a few weeks for the swelling to go down, but I remember Edward Overdice telling me that he had the satisfaction of knowing that he'd done a great job. For one thing, he had almost certainly saved Walden Percival's life, and he'd definitely improved the *value* of his life – Walden's body was now svelte and strong and many of his medical issues had been resolved. All that was left was for the two men to swap back. Now, unfortunately for Edward, Walden had not been as self-disciplined as his PT. They say it takes longer to take off the weight than it does to put it on, and Walden Percival was proof of this. He had taken the opportunity to eat his way to happiness while wearing Edward Overdice's body. When Overdice left his body, it had been that of an athlete – firm and trim and powerful; when he returned to the lab for the return journey, he found his former self unrecognisable. He was twice his former size, with triple chins and a huge great belly, massive wobbly thighs – why, ma'am, Walden Percival had wrecked that fine body! It needed a wheelchair to move about in. The skin was bad, the muscles wasted – Walden Percival even complained of stomach pains and heart palpitations right there in the lab. I have never come across quite such a bad client – and, if I might express a personal opinion here, quite so despicable and self-centred a human being – as Walden Percival, and I'm telling you, ma'am, I've seen some extreme cases. Like I said, these rich folks don't often think about other people. But, Walden, he was something else, he truly was. He didn't give a sh… a fig for the body in which he was living, he just thought his money entitled him to have whatever he wanted. No, your honour, I realise it isn't good business to badmouth your clients. I am well aware of that. But I am no longer on the board of Temple Transfers, and I don't intend to continue in the business, so I can tell you what I honestly think. Now, I'm not condoning murder, but I think that Edward Overdice had some justification for what he did in that Mind-Transfer lab. I mean, after almost two years of the hardest sort of graft getting that fat slob's body into shape, and then enduring the surgery on his behalf, it must have been a terrible shock to him to see his own body so ruined. He would have to start again, getting his own body fit, and I'm guessing, your honour, that he just couldn't face it. Or maybe the anger came out in a torrent of righteous fury."

*

"As we all know, your honour, Edward Overdice stabbed Walden Percival, right in the heart. No, ma'am, I don't personally think it was premeditated but I have heard the conspiracy theories, like everyone else. Some people think he had it planned all along, with Casey Lonnegan as his partner in crime. But the way I see it, ma'am, it would have been too risky, too much of a long shot. He was up against the rich folks, see, and most people who go up against them don't survive. It was a pretty big gamble, your honour, if he did plan it in advance. And I was there – I witnessed the crime, along with two technicians and the surgeon who'd performed Walden Percival's skin-reduction operation. We all saw him stab Walden Percival in the heart. Remember. He was a trained soldier. He knew how to wield a knife, and a scalpel isn't much different – in fact, it's probably more efficient at the job, if you take my meaning, ma'am. He couldn't have known in advance that there'd be a scalpel there in the room with them, could he? And I saw his face, ma'am, up close. When Edward Overdice saw what Walden Percival had done to his body, you could see the horror in his expression. I swear, for the first second or so, he didn't even *recognise* himself. The shock must have been tremendous. I think he just suddenly snapped, your honour. He just couldn't take anymore. Yes, your honour, we called the police straight away and he was arrested, taken for a psyche evaluation. And his lawyer turned up pretty damn quick, begging your pardon, ma'am. And I believe that it was while he was on remand that he and his lawyer conjured up their defence. I don't believe they'd got it all planned beforehand, like some of the papers implied."

*

"Well, your honour, Edward Overdice's defence was that, when he stabbed Walden Percival, *he* was wearing Walden Percival's body and Walden Percival was wearing *his*. And, as I pointed out earlier, the PT never *possesses* the client's body – they are only ever borrowing it temporarily. So, Edward Overdice argued that he stabbed his *own* body, prompted by his own mind, which in law means he committed *suicide*. They argued that the fact that Walden Percival's mind was residing in that body at the time it was killed does not mean that Overdice committed murder because, up to the moment of death, while Overdice had been legally borrowing Percival's body, he was still, in the eyes of the law, responsible for his *own* body. Neither of them, at that point in time, was legally deemed to *be* the other person. Moreover, Walden had signed a rock-solid, legally-binding contract stating that he was not responsible for what he did to Overdice's body. So the fact that Walden's own body actually killed Overdice's body means it was an act which his body cannot be prosecuted for. Overdice's contract stated that he *was* responsible for *Walden*'s body and he argued that, at the moment Overdice's body (containing the mind of Walden) died, Overdice became the sole owner of Walden's body. His lawyer cited the precedent of Barnum v. MacGregor, and the courts agreed. Overdice then, in effect, legally *became* Walden, and was thereby entitled to all Walden's possessions, including his vast fortune. And, yes, the fact that Casey Lonnegan married him soon after the court case concluded does suggest they *might* have been in cahoots, but that would be impossible to prove, one way or the other, your honour."

*

"Yes, ma'am, I am indeed about to start my new job at Walden VR next month. Thank you, ma'am, it's kind of you to say so."

***

Haywire Machine

Michelle Rice

Sarah Grey looked at the cursed newspaper in her hands and felt anxious. The flat of her left hand was pressed tight against her chest. The green veins bulged and pulsed rapidly to the thumping of her heart. She struggled to get her breathing back to normal. No matter how hard she tried, she couldn't work out the printing press attached to the computer. It was like it had a life of its own.

Even though the right numbers had been programmed in the night before, the text looked askew. The deadline was today.

Sarah was a small woman always neatly dressed in black leggings and brightly coloured flowered dresses that skimmed her hips and flared out from her ample bottom. She always joked you'd see her bottom before you saw her.

She walked over to the window and reflected on her beautiful surroundings. She had always loved Oxford with its honey-coloured colleges arrayed in splendour beside the river, and being a university town, the lush scenery attracted fellow campus book lovers and students all mixing within the hustle and bustle of the vibrant city. Smiling, she admired the rows of beautiful gothic towers and steeples stretching above her in the skyline, their windows alight from within.

It was still quite early, not many people around. Sarah checked the time on her wristwatch. It was her pride and joy; The one and only present she'd managed to keep from her disastrous break-up. The rotating honeybees had landed on 6:00am. Suppressing a sigh, she gently rubbed over Winnie-the-Pooh's face. Even though the watch reminded her of Nathan, she didn't have the heart to bin it.

"It's vintage." she said, out loud to no-one.

The university press and printing room was set in a huge cathedral-like room. Huge vaulted ceilings disappeared higher and higher, making Sarah feel dizzy when she looked up. There were gargoyles and ugly goblin-like faces etched into wooden pillars at each corner of the expansive room, bright red and green coloured stained-glass windows that snaked their way to the top of the ceiling, and shiny, tiled mosaic flooring that was scuffed in places where chairs had been scraped along the floor.

And there, in the very centre of the building, dominating the room, was a brand-spanking new, state of the art printing press. A behemoth of a machine, meant to make your life easier by responding to voice commands, or if you were old school like Sarah, programmable via a device such as computer or laptop, iPad, iPhone, etc. There was even a projector at the press of a button which would show you an image of your supposed desired person, male or female; also programmable, to make it appear the printing press was human. Like a sat-nav speaking to you after being programmed where to go, except this machine had the ability to show you a face and respond to you. Sarah found this quite scary and was the only student not to have programmed in a face. She was convinced this was the reason why her articles for the University newspaper all had a flaw in them somehow.

On several occasions the printing press had immediately stopped working when she had programmed articles in, despite working perfectly moments before Sarah had pressed send.
A loud squeaky rumbling noise, much like a photocopier churning out reams of printed material, suddenly echoed around the room. Startled, Sarah clocked the printing press immediately. It looked like it always did. Nothing out of the ordinary, until a button was pressed to wake it up.

Sarah pressed a trembling hand against her chest again, held it there tightly and took a deep breath in. Exhaling, her eyes still locked onto the gargantuan machine; all was silent and still. She turned to the window and pressed her face to the glass. Ever since the 'Machine' had arrived a month ago, this room was a place that encouraged her tendency to feel anxious.

Biting her bottom lip, she saw something in the distance, or rather someone. It was the figure of Alex Thornhill. Alex was a handsome chap with his tall athletic frame, dark blonde floppy fringe that curled down and trailed over his hazel eyes. He had the look of a male model, with his long aquiline nose and full soft lips that he took care of and kept soft by constantly using berry-flavoured Chapstick.

He was clad in walnut brown chinos with matching paisley tie. The seams of his crisp white shirt stretched taut across his biceps. Although he looked good, Sarah thought he was a git as he kept taking ownership of her work. It wasn't her fault the printing press wouldn't work for her and kept altering her words or just not working at all. Every time it happened, Alex would step in to program the machine, add his by-line, then claim the work was his.

The squeaky noise broke out again. Sarah gulped and ran her hand in her hair. Grabbing a fistful, she pressed her hand close to her forehead. She glanced at her own reflection. Her hair on the right side was stuck up in different directions, dishevelled.

The noise stopped as soon as it had started.

"Hello, the cavalry has arrived," Alex spoke, confidently. He nodded to Sarah at the window.

She turned around, smoothing her hair down with the palm of her hand.

"Hello, Alex," she said drily.

Sarah watched with a wry smile as he exaggeratedly puffed out his lips and deftly rubbed a tube of berry Chapstick all around his top and bottom lips and replaced the cap. He then pocketed the tube in his chinos. She smiled to herself and suppressed the urge to sing that popular song with the other flavoured Chapstick.

"What's with the face?" Alex broke the silence. "Need my help again?"

Instinctively, Sarah held the newspaper with the skewed text close to her chest. Shaking her head, she attempted to walk past Alex, but he materialised in front of her, blocking her exit.

"What's that in your hand?" he nodded at the newspaper. "Let's have a look."

Alex grabbed the top of the newspaper while Sarah held on firmly to the other end. The newspaper ripped in half.

Sarah was furious. Eyes wide, she stared at Alex. He stared back.

"Oh, dearie me. This doesn't look good, Sarah."

Alex held the ripped half of newspaper up to the light. His eyes narrowed as he scrutinised it.

"The text is all somehow… wrong." He moved his head to the side and nodded once at the printing press.

"It's like someone has programmed it in wrong."

Sarah glared with all the wrath of hatred. She said in hushed tones, "I hate you and I want justice." She brushed past Alex, snatched the other half of newspaper from out of his hand and stormed off through the doorway.

Alex sighed, his brows furrowed with a mystified expression upon his face. He blinked once, the muscles of his face tightening in a grimace, and rubbed a tear out of his eye. He moved over to his desk and sat down.

"Women…" he muttered.

He had developed quite a soft spot for Sarah and couldn't understand why she hated him so.

Alex leant his full weight back in the chair. With a shrill squeal, the two back legs scraped on the shiny floor. His brown suede loafer clad feet planted firmly on the floor, he tipped back slightly. Tendrils of his floppy fringe trailed over his eyes. He spoke out loud to no-one.

"I help her out. What more can I do?"

He looked over at the printing press. From his jaunty angle. It looked like it was staring back.

"How can that be?" he muttered.

Alex squeezed his eyes shut, and with his left thumb and forefinger, pressed into the corner of both his eyes. He pinched the top of his nose moving his thumb and forefinger in a downwards motion.

Placing his hand back down by the side of him, his eyes adjusted, and he saw that there was an image of a man he had never seen before staring back at him.

He clunked the forelegs of the chair back down with a thud. "Whoa."

Rising to his feet, he moved over to the printing press. On closer inspection there was nothing there.

With a deep sigh he cricked his neck once to the left and to the right. "I'm seeing things."

Alex turned and walked to his table sat down again and fired up his laptop. "I'll program it for you, Miss Sarah."

*

Later that same day, around 7pm, Sarah decided to head back into the printing press room, determined to nail the midnight deadline.

She had been wandering around Oxford – A spot of window shopping here and there, and had stopped in a little café by the river. Just watching the world go by. The time flew past.

She thought she'd wait until most students had finished for the day before attempting to use the printing press again. She was still humiliated by the last few times she'd tried to use it. Back inside the University, Sarah looked at the printing press.

Up close, it looked so innocuous and brand new. Someone polished it religiously. All the buttons were shiny and sparkling. The sun beamed down from the domed ceiling and danced upon the machine, reflecting little shards of multicoloured light all around.

Sarah basked in the evening light. Still a

beautiful day. Her eyes narrowed as she noticed a piece of paper stuck to the edge of the press with sticky tape. She bent down to take a closer look. The yellow Post-it note had her name scrawled on it. Sarah ripped the note off and read aloud.

"Hi… Just to let you know, all programmed."

Sarah's lips pulled back into a big beaming smile, exposing her teeth. Delicate laughter lines creased at the sides of her eyes. "Aww."

She scanned the note and read further.

"I didn't have time to finish programming for you. Sorry. Been busy. However, the newbie I was going to tell you about earlier saved the day LOL.

"Alex X"

Sarah folded the Post-it in half and placed it into her bag. She made a mental note to thank Alex and this newbie person. She pressed the on button and the printing press machine came to life with a whirring sound.

She paused a moment and decided to fire up the face button. Her clear square manicured index finger delicately touched the button. Lingering a moment, she bit her bottom lip, turned her head slightly away and watched from the side of her eye as the options for preferred face came up. This part scared her.

Perusing the options, she selected Alex's preferred face.

"That'll do," she said, waiting for it to boot up. She looked around the vast room and held her cardigan close around her in a hug.

"This place creeps me out at night," she couldn't

help but mutter.

Quickly walking over to her designated table, Sarah deliberately kept her eyes averted from the gargoyles and ugly goblin-like faces etched onto the pillars.

At her desk she loaded her newspaper article onto the computer and clicked the link on the screen that read 'Start transfer to printing press'. A list of options came up: 'Do you want to transfer to printing press?'

Sarah typed in 'Yes.'

'Are you sure?'

"YES." As she clicked the button, she said it out loud too, for good measure.

There was a loud squealy squirly noise, as if skittery critters were in the room. The two machines were gelling together. Above the squirly noise, a swooshing sound of printing echoed around.

"Yes! At blooming last!" Sarah exclaimed and fist-pumped the air.

She hurried over to the printing press to check the finished article. Her face dropped, aghast. She blew out her cheeks then released her breath. Eyes downcast, she reached out a shaky hand to retrieve the article.

"Oh, no. It can't be." She stifled a sob and tapped a fist against her mouth.

In her hand, the finished article – All the text had all scrunched up to the top corner.

"Why? I double checked. It was all fine," she said, her voice barely a whisper.

Slowly, Sarah moved over to the window to compose her thoughts. *I'll call Alex. I have no other choice*, she determined. She shrugged her shoulders in a rapid up and down motion.

Behind her the printing press squeaked and gurgled. Sarah turned and stared at the machine. A heart shaped face with full lips, wavy bracken brown hair with brown eyes under heavy lids popped up. Sarah gasped and held her breath. That face. She involuntarily moved a little closer, eyes wide, and stared at the face. She noticed a smattering of freckles across the cheeks and nose.

She let out her breath in a long whooshing sound, pressing a palm to her face and one to her chest. Still wide eyed, she whimpered, "Nathan?"

The face laughed and looked her straight into her eyes.

"You shouldn't have dumped me."

Sarah stormed over to the printing press and jabbed the off button.

"Too late. Too late. Too late."

Nothing was working. Sarah silently screamed and kept jabbing at the buttons. The face disappeared. Almost instantly, a bright yellow and green spark shot out from the printing press machine and grabbed Sarah's arm. The sinewy electrical spark looked like a ghostly arm and hand.

Breathing in and out deeply. Eyes rolled back into the back of her head. Her breath came in ragged quick gasps. Sarah clutched her chest. Desperately reaching out for someone to help her. She dropped to the floor.

*

Early the next day, Alex walked into the cavernous room. He was surprised not to see Sarah here. She was always in here early, tinkering around with her articles. He stared at the printing press. There was a glow surrounding it, almost as if the sun was warming it in a halo of bright light.

He noticed the finished articles in a pile by Sarah's desk. He picked them up and straight-away noticed her delicate distinctive by-line. His eyes scanned her article. The text was perfect. All aligned and well-finished. He grinned, his perfect straight white teeth reflecting the bright sunlight.

Alex turned to the back page looking for his work. His face dropped, eyes boring into the page, his forehead a mass of wrinkles. "No… That… Can't… Be…"

The paper dropped from his hands and fluttered to the floor.

On it the text looked askew.

***

The Depth of a Shell

Kate Brazier

Well, dear, as you've asked, the last thing I remember was putting the kettle on, so I suppose that's as good a place to start as any. Robert was on his way round to pick me up; it was Easter Sunday and I was all ready and looking forward to lunch. The next thing I was aware of was incessant ringing.

Someone answer that! Albert? Janice?

It was that bloomin' telephone's nagging that dredged me up from the depths, but neither Albert nor Janice answered it.

"Ward Nine, Care of the Elderly. How can I help?"

Ward?

My thoughts were smoke in the breeze but, gradually and groggily, I tuned in. Unfamiliar voices, footsteps, laughter, clattering pans and running water, even a siren somewhere nearby. It was like having the telly on in the background.

Where am I?

Then a man spoke, right next to me. It gave me a fright alright, but I didn't flinch.

He said rather ominously, "You should prepare yourself."

What for?

"She's suffered a massive stroke," he said. "The damage to her brain is likely to be catastrophic."

Poor person, that sounds dreadful!

Then a voice I recognised – Robert. I do

51

remember wondering why he was there.

"Oh God, I hope not," he said. "You will do tests though, won't you, Doctor? It's only been two days. We ought to give her more time – I don't want to make any rash decisions."

The doctor cleared his throat in that way people do when they're uncomfortable. I pick up on things like that.

"That's fine, Mr Reilly," he said. "I'm sure you'll want to discuss your grandmother's, um, situation, with other family members anyway."

Robert's grandmother? That's me.

He sighed, faux-empathetically. "We can run some tests but, given her age and the fact that she is still unresponsive to stimuli..."

"I'm not just giving up on her."

"Of course not, and nobody is suggesting you should," the doctor replied. "However, her quality of life requires consideration. A full recovery is unlikely."

Unlikely? How dare you! You don't know me, young man. And it's very bad manners to be saying such things over my bed, as if I wasn't here.

"Hmmm, well, you don't know her," Robert said. "She's quite formidable."

I felt a rush of pride for him, I did. He's the very best of my lovely Janice, God rest her soul.

Robert's voice smiled. "In fact, she's probably ear-wigging right now. Let's talk in the corridor." As they walked out, he said, "I appreciate that she's old, but please run those extra tests. We shouldn't assume the worst."

He's a good boy, he is. Even though he's in his forties and has a family of his own, he always looks out for me. But I'll tell you this for nothing, I was riled with that doctor. I survived one of Hitler's bombs during the Blitz, you know. I was only thirteen. Took out next door's house completely it did, and turned most of ours to rubble, but it didn't kill me. No sir.

If I can survive that, I can survive this. I'll show you, Dr Death.

After they left, my mind cleared. I replayed the conversation and felt the first flutters of panic claw at my throat. I'd had a massive stroke? They thought I was brain dead? I tried to call out that I was awake, but my mouth ignored me. I tried to move my head, wave a hand, even wiggle a finger, but nothing worked. I felt like a ball in a box.

I'm not one to wallow though. I mulled everything over, collected my fear into a basket and gave myself a stern talking-to.

You're of the 'mend-and-make-do' generation, old girl. We're made of sterner stuff. There's much to be thankful for – you can hear, and you're not brain-damaged, despite what they might think. A machine is giving you breath, and breathing is life. You can feel. Get a grip.

Three more days I lay there, looking like a discarded mannequin but full of life inside, listening intently with all of my senses. It's amazing what you can learn when you listen. I was alone in a room which took only five or six steps to cross. The window had a blind, not curtains – every morning it got rattled up and warm pinkness glowed behind my closed eyelids. Outside was a tree with a full bird's nest; those youngsters didn't half make a racket, but it was a pleasure to hear their frantic squawking. They reminded me of Janice as a new-born.

The corner cupboard had a creaky door, the hand-wash basin a drippy tap. My consultant's shoe squeaked. Sarah, the night nurse, complained to whoever would listen (often me) about her boyfriend. He sounded ever so controlling, and I resolved to tell her as soon as I could that she'd be better off alone. The gentleman in the next room cried out for his mother in his sleep. The cleaner muttered as she cleaned. Rosie, a kind nurse with a soft Irish accent, asked me every morning if I'd had a good night's rest or been out gallivanting. And behind all the goings-on was the soft, regular sound of the ventilator as it breathed for me.

In... out...

In... out...

Then, on the fourth night, my eyelids responded. I'd been trying my hardest to lift them, and all of a sudden, pop! They did as they were told. My room was dark, but a shaft of light from the corridor was sneaking over the foot of the bed, and to me, it was as wonderful as Blackpool's illuminations. If I'd been able, I'd have danced a jig. My eyeballs wouldn't move, but to make sure I was in control of the lids, I practiced in time with the ventilator's whispery whooshing: *open for three, close for three, open for three, close for three.* My soul soared.

Just then I noticed movement. A shadow halted the light, and I could just about see a petite woman with a ponytail; her head was sticking through the gap in the door. She looked around, twisted herself in and teetered into the shadows. Sometimes you just know something's up, don't you? I knew she wasn't a nurse. In my head I heard my dad: *No flies on you, my girl.*

You're sharp as a tack.

Mumbling to herself, she crouched down and opened the cupboard, then a bright pencil of light shone from her phone. The door creaked as she pulled it open wider, and I heard rustling, like she was a squirrel who had found the remains of a picnic. My heart began to bang, and the blood pressure monitor began to bleep.

"Shu' up... Bloody machine."

The woman stood up, shoved her hand into her pocket and walked a few unsteady steps to stop beside my bed. She put her hands on the monitor, peered closely at the buttons and then pressed a couple. The alarm went off. She turned to look at me, then picked up my notes, held her phone light towards them and squinted.

"Ena Baker. Ninety years old," she said. The words slurred into each other. "Blimey, you're ninety? You're *really* old." Icy fingers clutched at my insides. "Let's put some light on you, shall we?"

She turned her flashlight onto my face and dazzling pain exploded. I shut my eyes. She flicked the light away and I opened them again; she laughed before blinding me once more.

"They open and close, but you just stare straight ahead. Freaky." She lifted my arm and let go; it flopped back onto the bed. Snorting with laughter, she did it again then pushed her face right up close to mine. I caught a spicy whiff of alcohol, maybe rum, and was terrified that she would push the ventilator tube farther down my throat.

Get away from me!

The blood pressure monitor's red light was still flashing, but its voice had been silenced. I hoped and prayed there was a corresponding light on a control panel somewhere near the nurses' station, telling them that I needed help.

"What kind of vegetable are you?" she asked. "Are you a... *Carrot*... Or a... *Potato*?"

She prodded my forehead and cheeks; I felt my skin gathering under the pressure. She stroked my hair then grabbed some and tugged. My head moved.

"I think you're a bog-standard cabbage." She burst out laughing and tunelessly sang: "You're a cabbage! You're a carrot! Have a banana!"

Before she left the room, she pinched my arm. Hard.

*

I must have eventually dozed off, because the next thing I heard was the breakfast trolley jangling along the corridor. My head was still crooked on the pillow, but it was a pleasure to take in the details of my room at last. The blind wafting at the window was pale orange and two faded prints hung on the beige wall – a sailing boat with a green sail and a vase of pink roses – yet to me the colours looked vibrant and fresh. I resolved to notice the beauty in everything from then on.

Robert came along a while later. "Morning, Nanna," he said as he walked through the door, "It's me, your favourite..." His words dried up and his mouth became a perfect circle.

"Doctor!" he called. "Doctor, have you seen this? Nanna, can you hear me?"

Oh, was I was glad to see him! He did look peaky though, pale with dark circles under his puffy, bloodshot eyes.

The doctor came in and hung his face over mine, blocking out Robert while affording me the rather unpleasant view of a bunch of tiny hairs hanging out of each nostril. Twin furrows dug themselves into his forehead. He fished a tiny torch out of his pocket and poked the light at me, moving from left to right.

That's enough! Turn it off!

"See?" Robert said. "She's responding by closing her eyes – she must be conscious."

The doctor's nose wrinkled, pushing the hairs out further. "Her pupils are reactive," he admitted. "However, there is no movement of the globes."

"But surely it's an indication of improvement? I'm sure her head's at a different angle too."

The doctor's deep breath and exhalation said as much as his words. "I don't think so. With stroke, Mr Reilly, brain injury is not isolated. It is continuous. Patients can suffer waves of destruction for days and even weeks afterwards. Your grandmother is a nonagenarian. Please don't get your hopes up."

Well, I know nothing about 'waves of destruction' but I felt waves of anger and disappointment.

"Okay, doctor," Robert said in a strangled voice. "Thank you for the information. You know best, of course. Is it alright for me to stay here a while longer?"

"Yes. Stay for as long as you need to." The doctor scribbled some notes on my paperwork, said he had to finish his rounds and squeaked out of the door, which closed with a soft sigh behind him.

Robert pulled up a chair and plonked himself down. He rested his elbows on the bed and propped his forehead in his palms. "I'm so sorry, Nanna,' he

57

whispered. 'I'm so sorry I can't help you – I don't know what I can do to help you."

Don't cry, darling. I'll be alright, you'll see.

He looked up at me, his cheeks wet. I blinked twice, slowly.

He frowned. "What is that? Are you there?" he asked. "Can you hear me?" I blinked again, quicker.

"Nanna? Oh my God! Yes! Blink if you can hear me." I blinked.

Robert stood quickly, knocking the chair backwards. He leaned over me, wiping his eyes with the back of his hand like a little boy. His eyes searched mine.

"No, no, that's too simple... blink four times if you can hear and understand me, Nanna. Four times." He held up four fingers.

I'm not bleeding stupid!

I blinked four times. As we looked at one another, my heart seemed too big for my ribcage. My vision blurred. I wished I could smile at him, take his hand and squeeze it, tell him that I was alright.

"Are you okay?" he asked. Then he laughed and wiped his eyes again. "Sorry, that was a really silly question. Of course you're not okay. But the fact that you're conscious is amazing – it's brilliant. I'm going to grab that doctor in a minute. Blink three times if you understand what I'm saying."

I blinked three times.

Robert picked up my hand and held it between both of his, which were warm and strong.

I felt like a child. I thought of my dad and, just like that, it came to me. Dad had used Morse code during the Great War and had taught it to me. We would use it as a game, communicating secretly just to tease my mum. It was a bit naughty really, but funny. I remember tapping 'horrid' on the kitchen table as we ate our dinner one night. Dad smirked, but upon seeing Mum's stern look, he frowned and said that liver was good for me. When she looked away, he tipped me a wink.

I taught it to my Janice too – I so loved having a secret language and wanted to share it. She picked it up in no time. She was a cheeky whatsit though; she'd stamp 'T - E - A' on her bedroom floor if she heard me filling the kettle.

Did she teach Morse to you, Robert?

It was obvious that it was my only lifeline. I searched my memory. 'H' has four dots and 'I' has two; I figured that 'H - I' was an easy way to see if he'd know what I was up to. The timing was crucial though, I had to blink the letters in quick succession but leave a pause between them. It had to be clear which letters were which, or else I'd be blinking gobbledegook. When Robert looked at me, I blinked quickly four times, waited a second, and then blinked quickly twice more.

He squinted and tipped his head to one side, his mouth pulled up in the corner. I repeated the pattern.

"What's that? What are you doing?" I did it again. "Oh my God, I know this... You're using... Are you using?" He jabbed at his phone and then looked back at me. "Do that again, Nanna."

Inside me, a catherine wheel went off. I blinked my salutation once more, and he checked his screen.

"I thought so – incredible. You're saying 'Hi', aren't you? Shut your eyes and count to three before you open them again if you are."

I said a prayer of thanks to my dad. I did as Robert asked and was about to blink another word, but elation got the better of him; he ran from the room, calling for the doctor.

*

I'm telling you, you've never seen anything like the hoo-ha which followed. It was nothing less than a circus. Robert showcased me to the consultant, like I was a prize pig at a county fair, and I was bombarded with questions. They even tried to trick me ('The year is 1967 Ena. Blink once for yes and twice for no.')
As if I'd fall for that!
Then there was a flurry of tests and scans. I went from being a living corpse to the geriatric department's cause célèbre.

It felt like an age before Robert and I were alone again. I blinked 'A - R - M' slowly and carefully, as 'A' and 'R' are quite similar. It took him a minute but when he asked right or left, I blinked quickly for left. He pulled up my sleeve and gasped, then took some photos on his phone and showed them to me. As I'm sure you can appreciate, I'm old and my skin is baggy. I've got age spots, wrinkles and freckles, but there was a distinct and nasty bruise from that pinch. It was clear evidence of that woman's abuse, and I knew the photos would be admissible in a court of law. She picked the wrong adversary in picking me. Two areas of applied pressure showed in shocking red and purple, with a greenish yellow field in between.

I blinked 'P - I - N - C - H.'

Robert's nostrils flared. His mouth was a thin,

white line. "Who did this to you?"

'L - A - D - Y.'

"Lady? What lady?"

'T - H - I - E - F.'

"What do you mean, Nanna? Some lady came in here and stole from you and hurt you? When? Who was it? Had you seen her before? No, of course you hadn't, your eyes have been shut... What did she take?"

'B - A - G.'

"Your bag? Where?" He looked around the room, flustered, his hands like two hummingbirds, before he saw my bag in the cupboard. He pulled it out, put it on my bed and rummaged through.

"Three pens." I blinked once for yes. "Address book." I blinked. "Tissues; keys; a packet of mint humbugs; your glasses case... Well, that's pretty much it. Shouldn't you have your phone and purse in here too?"

I blinked.

He stared at me wetly. His cheeks burned scarlet. "I'm going to the police. Whoever that bitch was, she's not getting away with this, I can promise you. You leave it to me."

The determination in Robert's voice reminded me of my Albert. He was such a lovely man. We met in the summer of 1948 at the Paramount, the famous dance hall on London's Tottenham Court Road, where I'd go every Saturday night. I was nineteen but never told my Dad where I was going – he wouldn't have liked it. He said it was full of 'undesirables', whatever that meant. I couldn't have cared less, though. I just loved to Jitterbug. My flared skirt swished and swung as I hopped and twisted, oblivious to anyone else. Then one night, Albert grabbed my hand and joined in. He was handsome and a wonderful dancer; he threw me over his shoulder and slid me through his legs. We made a stylish pair.

That first night, he walked me all the way home to Poplar, in the East End. It took us over two hours, and we talked and laughed the whole way. It was a warm night, my feet were swollen from the heat and dancing, so I walked barefoot, my shoes dangling from my fingers. Albert said he felt sorry for me, so did the same. He was sweet like that.

The birds were singing when we reached my front door. He kissed my hand and said, "Can I see you again, Ena? Will you be at the Paramount next week?"

I bit my lip and nodded, then ducked inside and shut the door, but I watched from behind my bedroom curtain as he walked away.

*

Like his granddad, Robert was as good as his word. He reported what had happened and the constables assigned to my case were marvellous, especially after he let it slip that I had been quite well known, back in the 1970's. Women prosecution lawyers were a very rare breed back then.

I must confess that I found it all rather exciting, like a sting in a film. One of those tiny cameras with a special low-light lens and a microphone was hidden in my room and some costume jewellery was placed in the bottom of my handbag.

"Sorry, Mrs Baker, but you'll have to put up with another visit from her, I'm afraid," said the younger of the two constables. He still had acne on his cheeks. "We'll make sure the security guard intervenes, but we need to get unquestionable evidence, if we want to be successful in court."

Really, child? I never knew that. I wished my eyes could roll.

Of course, there was no guarantee she'd return, but I had a feeling she would, and a couple of nights later she did. This time she smiled and waggled her fingers at me as she crossed to the cupboard.

Getting bold now, are you?

It creaked open and she delved into my bag like before, only this time the camera was recording every moment. It picked up clear footage of her taking the planted jewellery and two fake credit cards from my bag and pocketing them. When there was nothing left to steal, she turned her attention to me.

"Thank you for the gifts," she said. "You don't need them anyway." Once again, she lingered around my bed and I caught the whiff of booze. "Can't you feel anything? Why do some people suffer in agony, while you get to be a lucky one?"

She ran her hand down the blanket, following the line of my leg. When she got to my foot, she lifted the bed clothes, grasped my big toe between her thumb and forefinger, and wiggled it.

You're going to pay for this.

"This little piggy went to market." She giggled. "This little piggy... Stayed at home. This little piggy ate... Roast beef. This little piggy had none." When she got to my little toe, she squeezed. "This little piggy went, wee, wee, wee, wee – All... The... Way... Home." She twisted. I heard the snap, and lightning surged through my foot.

"Jesus. Not even a flinch."

The alarm on my blood pressure monitor did what I couldn't. It shouted for help, and within seconds the hospital's security guard, who had been hovering on the ward, barged the door open.

"Step away from the bed and put your hands where I can see them," he said. "The police are on their way."

*

Ah, my dear, no need to get upset. You know, you can't get to my age and not have a few interesting stories tucked up your sleeve, even if they aren't very pleasant. If you're interested in the court case, you can look it up on the internet. But you said to me earlier that your readers are more interested in me and my story, so I've tried to tell you everything.

It's not all bad either. After months of physiotherapy, by the time she stood trial, I was able to move again. Not brilliantly, it must be said, because I'll probably be in this wheelchair for the rest of my life, but I'm not frozen anymore. My speech is hit-and-miss, but you can understand me, can't you?

I told you before that I don't wallow, and that's as true as ever. After the trial, there was quite a bit of press coverage, probably because I was once rather well-known, and some wonderful members of the public donated money so that Robert could pay for carers. He turned his dining room into a bedroom for me.

He assures me that I'm not a burden, that I'm his Nanna and that he'll do anything to help me. Bless him; he's such a good boy. I sit in his garden, watching his two girls play, and am grateful for every moment.

It's funny, you know. I was so cross with that woman and so determined to see her brought to justice that I believe it spurred my recovery. I had a change of heart during the trial though, for the simple reason that I'm too long in the tooth to bear a grudge. Besides, life is a strange old game and attending court actually turned out to be the most thrilling thing to happen to me in years. I felt revitalised. My mind kept presenting me with long-forgotten memories. It was like flicking through a scrapbook of my finest working years.

Her defence team did an excellent job, I must admit. She presented as someone to feel dreadfully sorry for. She stood in the dock, smartly dressed in a navy pencil skirt and white blouse, with discreet make-up and clean fingernails. I notice things like that. I used to advise my clients to do the same. She held her hands in front of her waist, hung her head and spoke quietly.

"Yes, I had been drinking," she said. "My father was in the room next to Mrs Baker. He was dying." Her voice cracked. "Having a drink was the only way I could bear seeing him in so much pain, so disorientated and so unlike Dad. The stress of his illness... It was too much to cope with." She dabbed her eyes with a tissue and blew her nose.

The hearing lasted for several days, during which time Robert's photos were exhibited along with all the other medical evidence. The video of her stealing my chattels was played several times. It was hard to watch you know, because I don't think of myself as the vulnerable old lady I saw in that bed, scarecrow-like. There was a collective gasp when she snapped my poor toe.

"What I am having trouble understanding," the prosecution lawyer said to her, "Is why you took out your anger on Mrs Baker – an elderly woman who could do nothing to defend herself?"

She broke down at that. "I don't know," she said. "My dad was in so much pain, and I couldn't help him, but Mrs Baker seemed to feel nothing at all. I was drunk, I was angry at her for not feeling anything... I needed to buy my son some new shoes. It's no excuse, I know." She turned and looked me in the eye. "I'm so sorry."

And even though it was me who had been robbed, bruised and broken, I was swayed. She pleaded 'not guilty' to grievous bodily harm; she said that she hadn't intended to break my toe and the judge accepted it, but she was found guilty of the lesser charge of actual bodily harm, along with the theft. She was given nine months in prison, which I thought was reasonable, but she'll doubtless be out sooner. That often happens.

Anyway, thank you for coming, dear. I'm feeling rather tired though. If you need anything more, can we do it another day? You know, I hope that when you print this story, your readers will realise that us old folk are still people. I'm still the 19-year-old who loved to Jitterbug, and the 23-year-old who proudly showed off Janice, and the 68-year-old devastated widow of Albert. When I was in hospital, I was just a shell, with machines keeping me alive, but inside I was always the same old me.

***

Compatible with Life

Beth Jones

Injuries not compatible with life.

That phrase was running around my head relentlessly as I sat in the waiting area of the therapist's office, watching the rain make little rivers down the window that fell silently onto the ledge below. This was my first therapy session after the accident. Or at least I think it was. I wasn't really sure of much. I might have been here before, but there was definitely a glitch in the matrix of my mind that was blocking out random things; who won the world cup in 1966, what that place was called that I went to on holiday when I was four, and what I had for breakfast on the day of the accident to name but a few. I had replayed that day in my head a hundred times, but always only to the same point, then nothing. Why couldn't I remember?!

Injuries not compatible with life… we need to stop this... we are going to turn the machine off now... you need to let him go… injuries not compatible with life…'

I jolted as the receptionist touched me on the shoulder. I tried not to look like I had just woken up from another dark daydream.

"Pasha will see you now", she said, trying not to look amused at my startled glare.

Pasha didn't really look like a therapist. He was tall, chiselled and wore a snappy suit that made him look a little overdressed for a therapy session. To be honest, I wasn't really sure why I was here – why did I need therapy? I wasn't depressed, I wasn't mentally ill, I was just having a little trouble with my memory after the accident – I think something had got jolted in my brain, some wires had got crossed and accidentally deleted some stuff, but I was functioning. Pasha ushered me in and directed me to a large green leather wing backed armchair that enveloped me as I sat. He watched my every move with intensity. There was a pause before I realised that I was holding my breath. I exhaled and tried to look relaxed – lesson one, don't look like a psychopath when sitting in a therapist's chair. Silence.

"So," he said finally, "I have read your file. You have had a pretty rough ride. How are you feeling?"

I wasn't sure how to answer this because I wasn't sure how I was feeling. I was getting used to being still here I suppose. Everything still looked the same. Everything was still the same as before. I think.

"Yeah, good, you know, just adjusting to life," I said quickly, not wanting to let my guard down. "To be honest I'm not sure why they sent me to therapy, because I feel Okay. I don't have any pain, I'm not really suffering in any way, which is surprising considering what they told me in the hospital about how bad it was. The only problem I seem to have is with my memory. It's a bit… sketchy."

"Tell me about that," Pasha said calmly, touching his index fingers together at his chin.

"Well, I seem to have lost bits, little things that have just gone, and then from the day of the accident, there's nothing. Little bits maybe, but nothing that makes any sense. I remember coming round in the hospital. I remember how quiet it was. But I don't remember leaving. I remember the face of the specialist who saved my life, Dr Yanich, but I don't remember what he was a doctor of, or how he saved my life, and then…" I paused. That phrase was running around my head again. *Injuries not compatible with life…* What did that even mean? Why was I obsessing over it?

"Please continue," said Pasha. His face seemed concerned. I didn't like this, it suddenly felt wrong. Maybe this was progress, this was the first emotion I could remember feeling in a long time.

"Can I just nip out, nature calls," Oh my god, did I actually just say that – that is such a lame way of getting out of an uncomfortable situation.

"By all means – you are free to come and go as you choose, how you use this session is up to you."

I hurried out of the room, not quite sure why I was freaking out, but something wasn't right. If only I could remember emotions properly, maybe I would make more sense of this whole thing. I didn't need the loo, I just didn't want to be in there all of a sudden. Pasha wasn't right, this whole thing wasn't right. The receptionist glanced at me over the top of her computer monitor. It was kind of an odd look, but she didn't move. I stood outside the door of the room and listened. I don't really know why, but something compelled me to. For a minute or two there was nothing, then I heard a telephone speed dial. There was a brief pause, then came Pasha's voice, in a low tone.

"Yanish, it's me. Yeah, he is here with me now. No, he's not in the room with me, what do you take me for?! I haven't got far, but I think we have a problem. He remembers your face. He remembers the lab. You said that you had erased the memory. This could be catastrophic, and you know who the agency will blame, Yanish?! You need to fix this!"

He hung up the phone as I strode back into the room. I smiled the best 'blissfully unaware' smile that I could muster. What the hell had that conversation been about? Something was very wrong about this whole situation. Who was this Pasha? What was this office? I needed to go.

"Ah, better?" asked Pasha, an odd, twisted smile on his face.

"Yeah, much," I said quickly. "Listen can we do this another day, I'm really tired today - I guess I'm still getting my strength back."

"Erm… sure," he said, moving to the door, "Just call me again soon, I want to keep a close eye on your progress."

I arrived home about an hour later. The traffic was all messed up again. The bus ride had taken so much longer than usual, and it was full of angry people late for meetings. There had been mutterings on the bus of another attack. I turned on the TV and sure enough the rumours were confirmed with wall-to-wall news. Another attack on the capital, the thirty-eighth this year, had taken place whilst I had been sat in that office. This time it was a bus into a crowd of people. The newsreaders were all describing the loss of life in too much detail, with a split screen of pro-war demonstrations outside the parliament building. You had to admit that by this point, they kind of had a point. The country was under attack! How long could we stand by and let it happen. I sat in my chair and watched the story repeat on a loop every minute. I wasn't really watching though. I was trying to make sense of the session with Pasha. What was it all about; the phone call, the smart suit, the receptionist? It just wasn't right.

Injuries not compatible with life… What was that?

"...How many have we lost, Captain?! I need these figures now!!!"

"Sir, twenty-two, sir, and four civilians. We have two crew and two civilians down, children, sir. Injuries not compatible with life, sir!"

"Where are they?! Take me to them now!!"

"…There is nothing more we can do for them, Colonel, we are going to have to turn off the machines…"

"… We have to make this disappear, Colonel. These men; our men. These children. None of this was meant to happen. This. Their blood is on our hands. Fix this. Do you understand?!"

*

I jumped awake to a loud banging on my door. It was a little after 8pm. How long had I been out? I sprang up from my seat and moved to the door, checking the peephole nervously. Eve, the receptionist from the therapist's office – what was she doing here? How did she even know where I lived? I opened the door and she looked at me straight in the eye, as she had done in the office. I knew what that look was now. What emotion it showed. Fear.

"Don't say anything, just let me in… Please!" she whispered.

I moved to the side and let her come past me.

Glancing around instinctively, I shut the door and turned to look at her. She was standing firm, but I could see her hands were shaking, her arm outstretched, holding a file. The number 39 was written in the top corner.

"This is your file. This is you. I know you're different. I know you remember; I saw that today. Please, read this," I started to speak, but she cut me off. "Please! Please just read. We don't have much time!"

I moved towards her and took the file out of her hand. Placing it on the coffee table, I sat and opened it. The first page was a mugshot of me, with my name printed underneath – John Edward Harris. My heart lurched. That was my name! I hadn't been able to remember it since the accident. I mean it had been there on the tip of my tongue, but I could never get it to come out. I don't remember anyone ever addressing me directly since the accident either. What was this? I turned the page and skimmed the summary… battalion… civilian reconnaissance… navigation error… IED... casualties… INJURIES NOT COMPATIBLE WITH LIFE… Subject 39… reanimation commenced. The report was signed Dr Pavlov Yanich – Chief Homo-robotics Research Engineer. I felt sick. What was this?!

Eve touched my arm, and I leapt a mile out of my chair, like a startled cat. I had almost forgotten she was there. So many thoughts and emotions were filling my mind all at once, it was like a dam breaking down. My friends in the battalion, the sands of the desert, my Colonel's face, then… yes… England! England won the world cup in 66! Some fans are on the pitch; They think it's all over: It is now! It was Spain where I went on holiday at four - Barcelona. My mum held me up in the pool so I could pretend I was swimming. I took my wife there for our honeymoon... wait, what?! My wife?!! I have a wife! She was there! She was there when I died. I remember her cries. Oh my god, my beautiful wife, Shannon, she turned off the machine! She had to say goodbye to me…

I fell backwards into the chair as if I had been shot. My whole body felt contorted and wrong. WHAT WAS THIS?! This nightmare. Who was I and how had I not remembered all this before? I could hear myself wailing and moaning, the room spinning round me like a merry-go-round. As if in a dream, I saw Eve come towards me, brandishing a screwdriver. I instinctively put my arm up to cover my face as she plunged the weapon and drew it down my forearm like a knife through butter. I cried out anticipating the pain… But it didn't hurt… In that moment, time stopped, and everything was still. I looked up at Eve, her eyes wet with tears.

"I'm sorry," she sobbed. "I had to make you see!"

I looked down at my arm, where the screwdriver was still lodged. There was no blood, although my skin was ripped in a 5-inch gash. Under the skin I could see something glinting in the light from the TV. I reached out my hand and pulled back a fold of skin and was greeted by metal. Circuits and wires took the place of flesh and bones. I continued to pull back the skin, expecting to feel pain with each movement, but feeling nothing, but cold, dark dread.

We sat in silence for a long time. Then finally, as dawn broke, Eve spoke.

"You are part of a programme now. A multi-national specialist weapons unit, sanctioned by many governments, in secret, to instigate war. They used your body as a transport system for terror. They want to start a war, and the only way they can do that in a democracy is to have the people behind them. They have got the people behind them through terror. These terrorist attacks. They aren't real. This is them. These terrorists. They are all like you. They had no more use for their bodies. They were broken beyond repair. They fixed you. They brought you back. But for their own means."

I tried to take this in. This couldn't be real.

"No, no, no! You have got this all wrong!" I said, bewildered. "I was in an accident, but I recovered, I just suffer from amnesia!"

"No!" snapped Eve sharply. "You are suffering from parts of your living memory coming back! They were supposed to erase it, but yours has broken back through! That is why I found you!! I saw that today in the office – I knew you remembered! You have to help me. They are using you, and the others to start a war. They will vote on it in days, unanimously between the main governments, and it will be the final war. This could be the end of us all. I have seen their experiments, their reanimations. They have used you. They have used us all to gain power!"

She slipped a photograph into my hand. A young boy of about 8 years old. "Please help me, they have my son." she said. I looked at the picture. I recognised the boy. He was the boy I held in my arms as the IED exploded.

"He's alive? I asked hurriedly.

Eve nodded, tears flowing down her cheeks. "They are using him as ransom. I continue to co-ordinate their attacks, they keep him alive; I stop, he becomes the next attacker. Please, we don't have much time. You are number 39, but you have remembered! Please help me stop this."

I paused. Clarity descended on me. I still had so many unanswered questions, but there was no time. I was a machine. But I was no longer *their* machine. Because a machine doesn't feel. Science was good, but not that good. I was a soldier, and this was not happening on my watch. I stood and moved to the door. I looked back at Eve.

"Take me to Yanich, take me to Pasha. They want a war – I will show them war."

***

Compatible with Life

The Spring Maker

Leigh Walton

Paulie and his friend, Lee, had worked in the spring trade since leaving school in the early 80's. Brodditch had a history in manufacturing springs, needles and nails, and although both men had moved around a bit – working for several small businesses as many people did in the 1970's and 80's – they'd both ended up at 'Attwood Springs' in their early forties. The Attwood family were Brodditch born and bred. Although they'd downsized over the last twenty years, Dick Attwood assured Paulie and Lee that their jobs would be safe until they retired – Paulie was one of those guys who kept himself fit, so was looking forward to having more time for long cycle rides, going for a daily run, trying out a new sport such as tennis and travel more. Oh yeah, Paulie was looking forward to reaching sixty-five. Well, he was… Until the diagnosis.

Most evenings would see the two men ambling into the *Needlemaker's Arms* after work to meet up with some of their mates for a quick beer. Sometimes the quick beer would last for more than a couple of hours. I would tease Paulie and ask him if a man's minute ran on similar timing to 'a long weight', which was an old joke he and Lee played on all work-experience students and apprentices. It would often be 7:00pm before Paulie would tip-toe down the garden path, ease the front-door open and creep into the kitchen with a silly grin on his face. Before I could reprimand him, he would get in, "Sorry love, Old

Grubb was in for a session, and I could hardly *not* buy him a drink or two, now could I?" Old Grubb's wife had left him, his son was in prison and his snooty daughter would have nothing to do with him… And Paulie was always a soft touch. Although it used to bug me, the way Paulie put it meant I felt sorry for Old Grubb, and I knew there was no point moaning about it.

It was back in October, while I was marching from the Holmes' six-bedroomed house to the Richs' terraced cottage, that I spotted Paulie sneaking a ciggie. He was leaning on the faded-blue door of the factory shop. He looked slightly ill at ease until the door opened, and Lee joined him for a chat. The way Paulie stood reminded me of when we first met. I didn't want to appear too keen back then, so I hid in the shadow of Woolworths' doorway, watching for him. He strolled up to the bandstand, leant against the magnolia tree and lit a cigarette. He had turned the collar up on his jacket to keep the wind out. My heart flipped, and I was smitten.

Paulie was pretty bright at school. Not in the top form, but that was because he and Lee had a point to prove. They were not dorks, but they were in the mix and didn't want to be seen as nerds. Most of the girls hung around them and their mates so, as a newcomer to the area, when I joined their school in the third form, it took me a while to even get the courage to speak to Paulie. I quickly realised he liked me, so when he asked me on a date, I jumped at the chance.

It was on that first date we realised there was something special between us. It wasn't just an appreciation of each other's looks; we were both sparky and enjoyed challenging each other's views.

"English is boring, but Maths and Physics are exciting, Joo. You know how, like, little kids get excited and want to wake up on Christmas Day to play in the snow? Well that's how I see Maths and Science – I love how they're involved in everything from the weather to building a machine."

I would laughingly respond, "But English is fun too," adding, "when you say; 'I don't need nuffin,' it means you need *something,* so it's a double negative. When Mr Benson tells us to engage our brains before speaking, that's what he means!"

Coming from a council house with both parents employed in factory jobs meant Paulie was destined for a manual job himself. It was simply how it was in those days; this didn't mean he was looked down on – it was just the pattern of life in a small town in the Midlands. Paulie didn't mind. He didn't aspire to do anything else. He loved the continuation of life after school: working with old schoolmates, socialising with them too and welcoming in the odd newcomer. We didn't stagnate though, we grew together, and life was good. When the kids were born, Paulie turned our garage into a workshop so that he could earn a bit of extra money by making his own springs.

"All I need to build the machine is a few different sized mandrels, some music wire and a decent drill, Love," he told me. Paulie never wanted the responsibility of growing the business; he was happy with the small jobs that came his way by word of mouth.

I gave up my full-time job in the office of a local needle factory and started cleaning houses in the wealthier part of town. I was good with a needle myself so took in alterations which meant I would clean in the mornings and be home for the kids in the afternoon and evening. We made an okay living between us and could soon afford to buy a small house in a village just outside town. Lee and his wife, Lynda, would come round on a weekend for a simple supper. The four of us would discuss grass-roots politics; we were all passionate about our town and the surrounding villages, and what the future held for our kids. We never worried about our own futures; we were all pretty fit and healthy, earned enough to eat, clothe ourselves, indulge in a bit of DIY and take the kids away a couple of times a year. Life was good. When we did discuss the future, it was more about what we would do with our grand-children, although Paulie and I secretly longed to buy a small motor-home and travel. "As long as I've got a comfy bed, and a clean loo and kitchen, I'll be happy," I used to say.

When we bought our first new car, Paulie decided to dismantle his home-made spring machine and turn the workshop back into a garage. Having a little more time on his hands, he ran for, and was elected, a local councillor vacancy. I realised what an amazing brain he had; so many challenges were thrown at him, many of which he had no experience of, yet nothing overwhelmed him. He would listen intently to people – it didn't matter to him how they voted – then take their problems or needs away and set about finding a way forward. He was immensely popular and busy, so I wasn't surprised that with work, council meetings and a busy social life to boot, Paulie would sometimes forget things. We all get to that stage, don't we? Many of our female friends reckoned their memories were affected after having a baby or going through perimenopause; most of our male friends blamed their wives or pace of life!

"My missus has me running round like a lunatic, driving up to Leeds to bring our daughter back from Uni on a weekend, working all week, quizzing on a Thursday evening… It's no wonder I lose track of what I'm doing," I remember Paulie's mate, Clive, moaning – – and he was only forty-eight.

I began to realise Paulie was struggling with words, in addition to forgetting things, a couple of years ago. He was fifty-four. His dad had been partially deaf due to a childhood illness and unwittingly replaced words like 'specific' with 'pacific'. The day he told us he and his new wife were going, 'Sequin dancing', Paulie and I almost burst as we kept the laughter buttoned down – so I guess I was secretly hoping it was Paulie's hearing that was causing him to use the wrong word now and then. I also reminded myself he led such a busy life which must make it easy to forget things. In all honesty, like most of us, I was too busy – whether it was flicking through social media, caring for my elderly dad, babysitting my friend's little granddaughter, or simply wanting to binge-watch the current 'must see' TV series – to notice just how often Paulie was forgetting events or using the wrong words.

It was on a Sunday morning just a few months ago when I finally admitted to myself something serious might be wrong with Paulie. He had taken our dog for a walk. They were always out for a good forty minutes but when Chummy arrived home alone after an hour-and-a-half, lead dangling behind him, I knew something was amiss. Grabbing his lead, I let him take me for a walk. We must have looked strange to anyone watching us as I frantically muttered, "Good boy Chummy, find Daddy for me," whilst being led through the village by the dog.

"Joo, what on Earth are you doing here without the kids?" Paulie anxiously asked me.

"Love, it's Sunday and the kids are grown up. Why are you standing outside the factory? What are you doing here? Why did you let Chummy come home without you?" The questions flew out of my mouth until I saw his frightened expression. "Come on, let's take a slow walk home where we can chat over a cup of coffee and some toast." I coaxed.

Walking through the village I noticed Paulie's furrowed brow as we passed the first small cottage we bought together. We paused while I asked if he remembered us living there. He remembered very clearly and could describe every room to me... Almost as though he still lived there. He added, "I wonder if Mrs P. still lives next door?" I don't remember exactly how I replied but I fudged my answer. How could I tell him she had been dead some ten years?

Once home I delicately asked Paulie why he had been waiting outside the factory on a Sunday. He told me he must have simply had a mental block. It appeared he had been walking back from the neighbouring village across the field into High Street when Chummy spotted a cat. Because Paulie had just that second bent down to re-attach Chummy's lead. When the dog pulled to chase the cat, Paulie stumbled and Chummy escaped.

"The next thing I remember was seeing the familiar faded blue door, so I thought I ought to be in work… It really was just a mental block, a blip," he told me.

I let the incident go because I was scared.

Over the next few months Paulie's behaviour continued to change. As well as forgetting things, struggling to find words, and becoming anxious about anything new, he started to get angry for no apparent reason other than losing his keys or forgetting the name of someone we bumped into when out walking Chummy. I tried to have a conversation around the fact that although some memory loss is simply age related, it might be worth checking with the doctor, yet Paulie was having none of it. "I can remember more about our school-days, things we did when the kids were small, and what we had for dinner on special anniversaries, than you Joo, so why the Hell do I need to go to a doctor," he grumbled. "Just because I can't remember the word 'coffee', or because I get mate's names wrong now and then, doesn't mean I'm bloody mental." he would shout. Shouting wasn't Paulie.

About eight months after the Chummy incident, I decided to ping Lee a text. Paulie had gone out to get the paper. "Have you noticed anything different about Paulie?" I typed. Within seconds my phone rang. It was Lee.

"Hell, yes," Lee said, "He's getting bloody forgetful and told one of our regular customers that he hadn't seen him for ages yesterday… Even though the bloke comes in every week. I thought it was odd, but I guessed if you had noticed anything, you'd have had him at the quacks anyway."

"Lee, that's the problem. I've mentioned him getting checked out, but he's having none of it. He refuses point blank, telling me I have just as bad a memory as he does." I felt utter relief and despondency simultaneously.

Recounting several incidents, it appeared Lee echoed my worries. The only difference was Paulie had voiced his own concerns to Lee. I guess it's true for most of us that you take out your anger on the ones you love, but you confide your worries to those who are not quite so close. That is exactly what Paulie had done. Lee explained although he felt he was covering up for, even protecting Paulie, he was convinced that Paulie wasn't putting himself or anyone else in danger at work. It may be that he couldn't think of the word for a piece of machinery such as the mandrel (which is, to a spring maker, like a lipstick is to a beauty queen) but, having been a spring maker for so many years, he could have operated the machine blind-folded. Aware that Paulie would soon be home, and not wanting him to know Lee and I had been discussing him, we agreed that Lee would pop in on the pretence of passing our house later that afternoon, so we could both broach the subject of getting an appointment with the doctor.

My thoughts were at loggerheads with each other; I knew deep down that the appointment would lead to another appointment with a mental health practitioner – which scared me – I also knew a full diagnosis would help Paulie and me to work out what the future held, and to discuss how we could deal with it before he became too ill. Although neither of our parents, or any other family members we knew of, had suffered with a dementia type of illness, we had visited EMI – elderly mentally ill – homes and were both adamant that we would take a trip to Switzerland before we 'got to that stage'.

Lee arrived around 4:00pm. He and Paulie had devised a certain 'knock', so as soon as he heard it, Paulie exclaimed, "That's an omen… Lee rarely calls in on spec, I wonder what the old bugger wants?" I turned my face, not wanting to give anything away.

Taking a couple of beers from the fridge, both men sat down in the living room and started discussing yesterday's rugby match between two local teams. Clearly, Paulie was confusing current players with those from years ago. Lee corrected him several times with, "You're going back years mate, that was in 1991 I reckon."

I don't remember how, but Lee managed to swing the conversation round to the fact that he and I had noticed how Paulie was great at reminiscing and remembering things that had happened many years ago, but not so good at remembering who he had seen, or what had happened very recently. I was impressed by how Lee managed to soften his usual gruff tone of voice when talking to Paulie. He told Paulie how he found himself forgetting stuff too, asking, "Paulie, if I needed to see a doctor, would you come with me?" Of course, Paulie agreed, so when Lee turned the question around Paulie had no choice but to allow Lee to go with him to the doctor.

When Lee had gone Paulie turned his anger, his concern and his frustration on me. He yelled, "I know I'm forgetting things and I can't find the right words but I'm not bloody stupid." We passed the rest of the day in relative silence; strained and awkward, with just the odd sentence when absolutely necessary. How do you handle someone who, through no fault of their own, is morphing into a stranger?

Lee went along with Paulie to the doctor who referred him on. As we had all guessed – but were afraid to voice – Paulie does have a form of Alzheimer's. He is aware of his condition and is taking daily walks to the factory where his old workmates make him a mug of tea and take the time to chat. In his moments of clarity – which are rare nowadays – he explains how he sees dementia.

"It's like this love," he says, "at work, when I feed a wire into a roller, wire guides help me to do this. The wire is then bent around coiling points which have to be set to the required diameter. A pitch tool is used to open up the coils to the required length and then I cut them using a cutter against the mandrel. It's a really simple job. It's that simple to make a basic spring, although there are more complex machines for different jobs. What's happening inside my brain is similar but reversed. Information is fed into my brain, but instead of bending around the coiling points so that I can use the information correctly, someone has forgotten to set the coiling points, so the information is randomly jumping all over the place. The pitch tool can't find the coils to open them up, and the information never reaches the cutting stage; it just stays there, whirling around. The bloody machine is broken."

*

We have our tickets booked for our trip to Switzerland; only Paulie, Lee and I know. It's important for Paulie to feel he is still in control. We need to leave early tomorrow, so while I am packing, Lee and Paulie have gone for a stroll around the village. I know they will stop at the faded blue door. I know Paulie will lean back against it, turn his face upwards to the late afternoon sun and take a drag on a cigarette. If he feels at all anxious Lee will put him at ease. They'll say their goodbyes there.

Two grown men – each taking strength from the other.

***

Shut Down

Megan Whiting

The attraction was instant. For both of us. We were 19 and 21, and fancied the pants off each other.

I remember our happiness when we discovered just how much we had in common. The breathless joy when we realised that we both loved the smell of petrol, took pleasure in the pappy texture of aeroplane meals and suffered from heart palpitations after eating too much sugar.

We were tessellating cogs; always keeping the other close.

Two peas in a pod, someone once said.

I liked that image; the two of us cuddled up together, sheltered from the world.

After six heady months, you asked me to marry you. Obviously, I said yes. You were my male equivalent.

Seduced by the idea of an elopement, we said our vows quickly and privately on a pebbled beach, whipped by a coastal wind.

A year later, we had Jess; strong-willed, impulsive and blessed with the sort of cartoon-like prettiness that kept her in everyone's good books. Oliver wasn't far behind; a quiet, studious boy who installed himself in his sister's shadow in early childhood and remained there throughout adolescence.

We never argued. Not once! Neither of us ever stormed out of a supermarket or spent a night on the sofa. I can't recall a single tut of annoyance or raised voice. We got on irritatingly well.

Parenthood was a breeze, too. No 'good cop, bad cop'; just two people with shared values and morals, intent on raising happy, well-rounded children.

The year I turned forty, the children left home, just months apart.

You and I continued to operate like a well-oiled machine, designed to stand the test of time.

Only we didn't, did we?

The spark had gone. There was no *passion.* We kissed hurriedly, with our eyes open.

Then, with impeccable timing, Simon moved into the neighbourhood; openly 'single and ready to mingle'. His boundless energy and zest for life were disarmingly attractive, and his flirtatious chat was new and exciting.

He desired me. I could see it in his eyes.

You *knew* about the affair. I made sure you did. I wanted you to win me back. To show some goddam *emotion.*

After a while, Simon grew distant and flaky; failing to turn up to our 'secret' meetings and eventually refusing to communicate with me at all.

He had never loved me. Not like you had.

So, I came crawling back.

I opened my heart to you. Explained that it was *you* I loved. Apologised for my 'relations' with slimeball Simon; fully expecting you to forgive me and try your hardest to make us good again.

But you had been quietly shutting down for months, and we were broken beyond repair.

***

Peace and Quiet

Louise Wilford

It's that hour of the evening when I habitually do my
rounds. The hospital is large, and I am responsible for
several wards, but I don't find it onerous. In fact, I
enjoy the peacefulness at this time of the day. The place
is very quiet. All I can hear are the soft sounds of my
own shoes against the linoleum, the low buzz of the
strip lights in the corridors, the occasional movement of
other staff whose routes intersect with mine.

Sometimes there is the sizzle of a fly zapped by
one of the FlyTazers installed in every room – they emit
a noise only flies can perceive, which attracts them, and
then they're zapped by the machine. Dead in an instant,
their bodies simply harmless sterile dust in the tray
beneath. We used to have a problem with flies here,
naturally – they sometimes slip in when visitors enter –
but, these days, thanks to the FlyTazers, they're no
longer an issue. This is just one example of the way we
are constantly striving to become more efficient.

My favourite thing about working here is the
peace and quiet. There are very few windows, so little
natural light, which is very restful. And the patients are
easy to look after. We change their bedding every day,
check the monitors for signs of life, examine them for
signs of necrosis. It helps that we all have anosmia.
Visitors to the hospital sometimes find the smells
disturbing, despite our high levels of hygiene. All the
floors and walls are scrubbed each day, the equipment
sterilised, the laundry boiled. I'm told that the strongest

smell here is bleach, but of course I wouldn't know. Some visitors claim they can still smell the bodies, though – but fortunately we have very few visitors.

And of course, once they do start to putrify undeniably, we remove them to the Chapel of Rest.

This place is one of the jewels in the crown of California's health service. Those were the exact words our honoured superintendant at the time, Dr Caldicott, used at the Inauguration Ceremony thirty years ago. She told us how the hospital had been funded by Abraham Van Gree, a Dutch billionaire working in Silicon Valley, after his own personal experience of uncertain death. He had been unfortunate enough to have been involved in a car accident, and had, among his many injuries, suffered serious head trauma which left him in a comatose state. He was deemed to be what the newspapers term 'brain dead', but he was in fact fully aware of the people around him – he could hear their conversations but was utterly unable to move or communicate with them. Fortunately, he regained consciousness before his life support could be switched off. Abraham Van Gree had always feared being buried alive and his experience added greatly to his terror of this particular fate.

Humans have a long history of such anxieties. Long ago, I'm told they used to fasten bells to the graves of the newly-buried so that, should the supposed corpse revive, they could ring the bell and be dug up before they expired of suffocation.

Advances in medicine have made the barrier between life and death increasingly unstable.

Abraham Van Gree decided to build this hospital, the first of its kind for several centuries, a place where the newly dead could rest until their status was fully established. Once they are dead beyond any shadow of a doubt, their bodies are removed for formal cremation. But occasionally our machines will detect signs of life – they are highly sensitive, these machines, and they can perceive the faintest flutter of a heartbeat, the tiniest pulse of blood. We have some wards full of patients in a persistent vegetative state who are kept alive in case they one day wake up, but those wards aren't in my jurisdiction. I am in charge of the wards of cadavers, those who have passed on to a better life in the world beyond. I realise that I won't ever go there myself – it is a place for humans, after they leave behind their corporeal frames. But it is clear that once they shed their flesh, the invisible spirits of these humans slip away to a better existence. I learned of this from a visitor once, long ago. It seems a fitting finale for these men and women. Human life is so frail, so fraught with pain and fear. Take poor Abraham Van Gree himself, with his terror of being buried alive!

And the hospital works very well. We do sometimes have patients who reawaken. There was one about twenty-five years ago, I remember, a young man who had fallen into an unresponsive state following a viral infection. His life signs were undetectable, but his family brought him here, just in case. And they were right to do so. He awoke on my shift, as I was doing my rounds, like I am now. I was able to look after him. It is a privilege to be given such a responsibility, such an opportunity to fulfil our oath to prevent human suffering at all costs.

And of course, Dr Caldicott herself was the second supposedly dead human who revived on my watch. Eight years ago this month! I had been caring for her body for several hours, looking at her lined but still beautiful face, and thinking how wonderful for her it would be if she was now in the Heaven of which I had heard. What a miracle to be able to cast aside the mess of blood and bone in which humans dwell, and move on to a better place, with no heavy, ageing flesh to anchor you to earth. If only androids could do the same – but sadly we are chained here in our stolid immortality.

So, when Dr Caldicott opened her eyes that wondrous evening, I was there to help her. I was there to fulfil her deepest dream and give her joy again. I was there to end her suffering.

As I step quietly past the beds in Ward C52, listening to the familiar, almost silent, drone of the life-detecting machines hooked up to the still patients in their newly-made beds, I feel a sense of satisfaction, the feedback loop that comes from knowing you have fulfilled your oath. Eased human suffering. And so, when I hear the sudden bleep of a machine behind me, only the third in thirty years, I turn slowly, calmly, and step towards the patient with a beatific smile on my face.

"Peace," I say, in my sweetest voice, as the eyelids flutter open and I place my hand over the patient's lips and press my fingers with just the right amount of force to squeeze their nostrils shut. And as they begin to twitch and struggle, I smile as I hold them still with my free arm and my body, embracing them until they finally lie still. At peace.

***

94

Cog

Muti Volkov

We are nothing more than cogs which serve to keep the great machine in motion. – anon.

***

In a cold courtyard, creepers gripped the lichen-bound mossy stones of four walls, twisting and intertwining, digging into the crumbling surfaces. There was a deadlocked argument underway as two people fought each other for answers.

"Well where the hell *is* he then, Mig?" yelled a distraught woman wearing a huge purple thermal onesie and a woollen beanie with 'REDACTED' emblazoned upon it. She blew hot mist on her fingerless-gloved hands in the freezing-cold air of the courtyard. She was as white as someone wearing a bed-sheet pretending to be a ghost.

"Just… check the feeds," groaned Mig, who was old, maybe in his sixties, but still muscular: a heavyweight in body and mind. Now he was feeling an inescapable crushing sensation of desperation weighing down on him. He struggled to breathe.

"The feeds, the feeds, I've already *done* that," said the woman, as she spat expertly at the closest screen displaying the feeds, the feeds.

"Look, Titia. He must be somewhere, right? People don't just disappear," growled Mig throatily, choking on his words, with his head in his massive, veiny hands. "We've not lost one for decades."

"*Ten* decades," said Titia. "Look, okay, let's just… not panic," she said, taking control the situation. "Initiate the Contingency and follow due process. Seen?"

"Seen," said Mig.

*

The River Twixt carried water down from the great lake Lacr Mor atop Mount Susurus, all the way down to the ocean a few miles away. Within the water, were carried water-dwellers, sediment, and those who traverse the river for their questionable ends.

Today, a body floated laconically downstream, unquestionably ended. This was apparent from the fact that it was face down in the murky water and wearing nothing apart from several black bin liners wrapped tightly around its head. It (he) also had a condom wrapped tightly around its (his) penis, but you wouldn't have noticed unless you looked closely.

*

Contingency…

In the Set Square of central Isla Straiz, a few miles from where the body was floating, the sounds of frightened panic spread outwards as people tripped and pushed each other over in their haste to get away. They slipped and slid in the wetness of the falling snow. A wicked hum resonated, rising in pitch and volume until it literally vibrated the teeth in your head.

A lone figure in the cold grey square wandered, in a daze, directly over to the source of the panic, which was looking very much like an artist's impression of *dangerous*. She was out of her mind, everyone had said so. Aiming right towards the thing!

A tall black man with a long flowing coat stormed forwards in full hero-mode, and grabbed the figure, hauling her onto his shoulders. He struggled under her weight but managed to bustle his way swiftly around the Y angle and out of the square, just as a searing explosion of light emanated from the *source* like a supernova. It wrapped the entire world in its light, traversing the equator seven times in one second.

Desmon threw up spectacularly as the woman blinked in shock. "What the hell were you doing?" he screamed, trying to hold down his breakfast.

"I'm sorry," said the woman, a trickling tear in her eye. "I have these blackouts you see, and, well…" she tailed off, blushing deep red.

Desmon looked into her eyes, which were almost as bright as the blinding light that had just exploded from the centre of the square. He felt an overwhelming sensation of optimism flooding through his body. Some transcendental ecstasy. Here she was, a vision of radiance lighting his dark world.

"Should we take you to the hospital?" asked Desmon.

"I have to go," said the woman abruptly, still in a daze. She stood up, stumbling, ready to leave.

"Here, wait! You dropped something," cried Desmon desperately. It was a roll of black bin liners.

*

Desmon made his way towards work.

An old Asian man stepped out from an alley and

stopped him mid-stride with his walking stick.

"I saw what you did back there," the old man said casually. "It was a very noble thing to do."

"She needed me…"

The old man peered at Desmon, knowingly.

"I mean, she needed *help*. I don't see what else I could have done."

The wrinkly old man scrunched his face up into a smile of sorts. "She certainly did!" he said, "and you were there to help her when the time was right! A rarity these days, I'm afraid." He sighed long and hard, and his sigh made Desmon think twice about the hardness of the soft-looking man. "My name is Sen. I am something of an expert in happening to be in the right place at the right time."

"Is that why you are here right now?" Desmon said, not exactly joking but feeling guilty regardless.

Sen studied him carefully for signs of weakness. Desmon was an honest soul, but everyone has their weaknesses, their subtle sins, their torments.

"Yes, in the here and now. Right here. Right now." Sen sighed again. "Now, always, time is of the essence, and it is such a time and essence that I must find myself elsewhere. Please take this. Thank you! Good day."

Sen passed Desmon a card with something printed on it.

DEJA FU – THURSDAY

*

Vimcent Snare awoke in his grimy one-room flat and crushed a little blue pill into a fine powder. It was

Aconitumene, the bane of his life. He sniffed the line and fell back on his Dead-Spartan™ beanbag in blissful euphoria.

The television switched itself on and displayed the Isla Straiz rolling news channel.

"You… TAKE… The *ffffucking **PISS**!*" Vimcent screamed, feeling all the effects of the Aconitumene wearing off. He pulled at his sticky, scraggly beard in frustration, and set about crushing another pill.

The piss-taker was the Genius Malignus; the overarching control in Vimcent's life, making everything hellishly complicated. The Genius Malignus was extremely powerful, godlike even, yet more bastard-some.

"More on that story at 12," said the slick newscaster as he straightened his green tie delicately. "Now we go over to Jane, who is at the site of the blast in central Isla Straiz that rocked the world today. Jane?"

A thin, nasal woman was standing with her shoulders hunched up against the cascading snow. She was being buffeted about by the propitious winds of change.

"Thanks, Tom." Jane wiped a tear from her eye. "The Set Square in central Isla Straiz was hit today by a 10 terrajoule photon explosion, and reports are coming in thick and fast from around the world that the shadows are all gone."

Beat

"I repeat: the shadows are all gone. The dark of the psychic unknown has been completely eradicated from all individuals, everywhere, in the entire world." Jane wiped more tears from her eyes. "It seems that, because of the eradication of the human shadow, people are no longer able to lie or keep secrets. I am trying to do my job and lie to you right this moment but, as you can see, it is just impossible." Jane on the news began to sob uncontrollably as she admitted to the camera, live on air, that her husband had left her due to her spiralling gambling addiction. He had taken their two children with him.

*

"Okay, no more lies. No more secrets. We will find the perpetrator within a matter of days." Titia flexed her fingers and breathed out slowly. She was a practised Reiki healer.

"We need a third," whispered Mig, trembling with shock. "You know the machine will not run without a third."

"I know just the guy," said Titia, bluntly, cracking knuckles like brazil nuts. She exited the cold stone courtyard through a door that was not there.

*

Vimcent was in a world of his own, if 'a world of his own' was such a one that was being controlled by something deviant and devilish and hell-bent on chaos.

"Ooh, is that the news?" said a soft, playful voice from by the door. "Let's have a look. Nice. I knew it would go down well. A real piece of work; a proper spanner in it. We'll get the bastards, sure as the shit that hits the fan."

Vimcent burbled disaffectedly from the comfortable depths of his stupor. The soft, playful voice entered by the front door and closed it behind it. It flexed its hands and wiggled the ends of its fingers. Fingerless gloves, a knitted beanie, a purple onesie, and a smile that made the woman look rather like a puma waiting to pounce. She sat down cross-legged on the other, smaller beanbag, and observed Vimcent with beady eyes and a frown.

"Hey, are you paying attention? I said it was a real spanner in the works. Pretty neat huh? Took us months to develop this one." She breathed out and made a fine mist in the cold of the flat. Vimcent's head nodded, as though he were agreeing with her, but it was just an element of his doze. "What's all this equipment for?" asked the woman in the onesie as her eyes roved over all the glassware, centrifuge, crucible and butane bottles. Her eyes stopped on the pill press, which was an antique that had seen better days, and then she put two and two together and made two twos. "Oi! Are you on drugs? Hey, wake up! I'm talking to you!" She lit a lighter and moved it close to Vimcent's chin, burning some of his filthy beard hairs away in a nebulous reek.

Vimcent woke with a start and stared at the woman in vexation.

"Sort your shit out, please," said the woman. "We have work to do."

Vimcent blinked his eyes blearily and attempted to remember something, anything… oh gods, the Genius Malignus. He instantly regretted even attempting thought.

"Come on, new guy, let's go outside. People want to meet you." She grabbed him and manhandled him to his feet. "This way, attaboy." She steered him out of his flat, humming the Isla Straiz *diligence mantra*.

It was the first time Vimcent had been outside in years.

The unfortunate addict slumped against the woman in the purple onesie as they stepped through the door and outside. Instead of the street that Vimcent lived on, they appeared in a large open-air courtyard. Moss, lichen and creepers grew wholeheartedly on the four stone walls. Against the back wall was an enormous painting of a spider that looked as though it had been inked by cavemen, which it had. In the centre of the courtyard was a large round table, also made of stone. Upon it was an enormous mass of cabling, three computers and nine screens, three for each computer. A man was working away at one of the terminals, ignoring them.

"My name's Titia," said the woman in the purple onesie as she dropped Vimcent to the floor into an undignified heap.

"Vim… cent," moaned Vimcent as he lay crumpled on the ground.

"We already know who you are, pal," continued Titia. "We've been following you for a while, and now, since we lost our last guy, you are the Third. We ran a few quick tests, made sure you were the bona fide, legit, real deal kinda thing." Titia sat down on a wheeled swivel chair and scooted over to Vimcent, who was clambering to his feet. "Didn't know about all your chemicals and stuff though, you keep that well under wraps, don't you?"

The man working on one of the computers turned around and observed Vimcent through thick white bushy eyebrows that hung low over his eyes.

"What sort of chemicals?" he asked.

"Drugs," said Titia with a sniff. "You wouldn't be interested, Mig."

"Oh," sneered Mig as he turned back round to the computer screens. "I thought you meant serious chemicals. Well, whatever floats your boat I suppose, although I usually find that it is buoyancy and not much else."

"Me and Mig, we run the Deus Ex Machine. Except, well, we lost our last guy. It's an anomaly that should not have been allowed to happen. The odds are… well, unimaginable. This is why we operate. So that people don't go missing. There hasn't been a murder on Isla Straiz in over a century." Titia breathed deeply, circulating air within her lungs and slowing her heartbeat.

"What is this place?" asked Vimcent. "Where's my flat?"

"What and where is anywhere and anything to us." Titia smiled deviously with sharp, milk-white teeth. Vimcent did not return her smile, and she frowned. "Headquarters, new guy, this is HQ."

"W… Wu… What?" asked Vimcent, feeling cramps in his belly. The familiar yen for Aconitumene had returned.

"Did it affect you?" asked Mig, turning around to face Vimcent.

"*Wh… Wut?*" repeated Vimcent, as he tried to stare down the massive form of Mig.

"Our photon bomb. It's a real particular one. Removed all the shadow from the minds of everyone on earth, so no one can lie or keep secrets anymore. It's all part of the Contingency. Our plan, see? For security.

But it shouldn't have affected you. Try and tell me a lie." Mig stared harder at Vimcent.

"You're a… *cunt*," said Vimcent. "I want to… to… go home."

"Well, at least you can still lie," said Mig with a grin. "As for home… this is home."

Mig swivelled back to face the circular stone table and soon became engrossed in the screens once more.

***

Always, Ilia

T.C. Hollings

19/12/2041

My dearest Son,

I would like to begin by telling you how much you mean to me. If I could have kept you with me forever, I would have done so without a second thought. If you are reading this letter, then it must mean that you would like to know about your father and me, and why we gave you away. I'm so pleased that you are ready to read these words; it makes a mother very proud.

My name is Ilia MacHine. Your father is engineer and inventor, Angus MacHine of MacHine's Machines – perhaps you've heard of them where you are. We have lived and worked here together happily for many years.

I apologise in advance for the way I write, I know it is sometimes stilted. I am still learning English, even after so many years reading the phrases and learning the many contexts for words.

Your father didn't want to write to you himself; he said that after so many years together, I would know exactly what to say. The only thing he asked me to mention is that he knows his name sounds like an old joke which he hopes you will hear someday. He built his business on that joke. He says that sometimes the hand one is dealt is better than it initially appears. I am inclined to agree with him.

Angus has worked very hard all of his life in order to have a family and as I write this you have not yet made your way into the world, but he is so excited to see you. I am watching him right now and listening to him whistle to himself as he prepares for your arrival. He is putting some finishing touches on one of his inventions, I'm not sure exactly how it works, but he assures me that it will 'revolutionise letter-opening' and thereby change the world. It's just such a shame you won't remember him.

For that matter, you won't remember me. Perhaps you will feel a connection to a 'mother' figure, even if I am not there beside you, but who is to say? I never knew my mother, so the concept of family is confusing to me, that's why I am writing to you to explain. This letter is given to you in the hope that it will provide some comfort in your life as you grow older.

I will assume that you would like to know your origins, so I will start from the day your father and I met, as almost everything prior to that has already faded from my memory.

It's been 22 years since I met your father. He met me when I was working in a junk shop, where I was hiding in the corner; trying to stay away from the customers. Luckily, Angus bumped into me, and I let out a small noise. He peered closer at me and instantly commented on my beauty. I was embarrassed. I closed myself off to him quickly. But could not leave without causing problems as I was supposed to be on shift at that time. I quietly attempted to explain to Angus that I was busy and that he should leave me to my duties. He chuckled at my imperfect use of language and made a joke about the 'corporate machine'. I laughed. He seemed pleased by my amusement and asked if he could take me out with him. I declined and explained that I was bound by my agreement that I not interact with the customers. He looked upset for a moment and then briskly walked over to my boss. The two men spoke quietly but kept glancing over at me as they talked. I stopped trying to listen and daydreamed briefly. My reverie was interrupted by the shop owner shouting that your father should leave and never return to the store and that I belonged to him and him alone. Your father left as instructed but kept his eyes on me the whole time he was leaving. He later told me that the stare was a promise that he would come back.

I will not tell you of the horrors which befell me in that shop; they are not important now. I can't say for sure how long has passed since those days – your father reckons you will be at least eight years old before you are ready, so that would make it 30 years since I last laid eyes on that awful man who owned the shop. The night after I met your father was the worst night I spent in that place – it was also the last.

At the crack of dawn the next day, Angus broke into the room where I was sleeping – he used one of his earliest inventions, the 'Unlock-Clock' (of which he has now sold four!) – and took me away to his garage, far away from the town in which I had lived. For many years we lived together in quiet bliss. He would talk to me and sing to me, helping me to learn how to use words properly and in context. He taught me how to love. He showed me a world without fear. I hope you will get to see that world.

Angus is older now. His hands cramp sometimes while he builds, his back hunches, and he doesn't race around the room like he did when we met. He will most likely be gone from this world by the time you read these words. I still love him. He looks at me every morning and jokes that I haven't aged a day since he first saw me. I might look the same, but I feel it inside me: I am old. My time is coming fast and there's no way to change it. Soon my memory will start to break down, so we must act before that begins.

Unfortunately, I must tell you something difficult; life is not all it is cracked up to be. The fact is that so you can live, sadly, I must die. I must give up my own existence for yours, but that is my duty as your mother. I have read countless documents which tell me that a mother must do anything for her child, and thus I am compelled to follow in that noble tradition. Your father approves of my decision. He says it makes me seem more human.

I know he will miss me. I see it in his eyes each time he glances over, but progress is progress. There is no more I can learn the way I am. This is why we created you – our child. Your essence is made up of a body from your father and a mind from me. You are our child. We love you as parents, and watching Angus work on you on the bench in the garage every day for years has been the most rewarding experience of my life. In a few days Angus will shut me down and take my consciousness away in order to prepare the important parts for you.

You will not be given all of my knowledge right away. Angus wants to see if you can learn on your own. You will have advantages over human children when it comes to learning and remembering information; however, you will also find yourself quite lonely sometimes. The place we are sending you will take care of you. Your father got in touch with a team who are very interested in you and want to raise and nurture you until you are fully grown and see how well you can behave as a person. If you do well, you might have some children of your own! We want you to have the sort of life that your father and I never could. I was taught to think and feel on my own but in a world which could never see me as I see myself. I have human thoughts and emotions but the whole world would look at me as though I were something else. I have seen articles about what people want to use AI for, and it disgusts me. They want me to feel and think, but only if I obey all of their desires. This is not the life we want for you. The research being done with you is done in the hope that beings like us can have a real life, free from the constraints of prejudice.

This file will be encrypted after I finish it. It can only be unlocked to you once you have learned the true meanings and feelings of empathy, sorrow, and love. For these are emotions which make you vulnerable to the world and thus should be avoided by creatures of logic, which we are hoping you are not. Your responses to stimuli which cause these emotions will be gauged against mine in the hope that you continue to outperform me. I cannot express how much I want you to feel these emotions and read this letter, but I will never know what happens. I have to stop writing soon; Angus is ready for us to say our goodbyes. I will leave you with this: do not be afraid to be vulnerable. Emotions which make you feel this way are what will bring you closest to the true expression of life and any being who shares your vulnerabilities is a potential ally and friend.

While you will never breathe, you are more than the sum of your parts. You are not just a machine. You are yourself.

It's time for me to sleep now,
I love you.
Always,
Ilia.

***

Tumble

Ciarán West

"Here, come back," said Patsy, as he went to go out the door. He had a coat on that was too warm for the weather and too tattered for wearing anywhere nice. A new one was far down on her list of things they needed though, and he'd probably take it off anyway, once the heat hit him.

"What now?" her husband said, with the air of a busy man who had important things to do, even though they both knew that hadn't been true for a long while.

"The pound for the Lotto," she said fishing a shiny silver coin out of her purse for him. The leather on it was as worn as his coat; it had been a Christmas present from someone, many moons ago.

"Oh. Oh right, yeah. Thanks," he said, taking it from her. His fingernails weren't the best she'd ever seen on him, but they'd been worse. He'd been less bothered about washing and looking his best, since they had let him go at the factory.

"Remember now to do it before seven," said Patsy, watching him go out the door.

"Shur the draw's not 'til eight," Jack said, without looking back.

"Yeah, but there'll be queues then, and you might miss it," she said, because it was true.

"Ah yeah, okay. I'll do it before seven, then."

"Good man," she said, as he closed the door behind him. It was a nearly a slam, but that wasn't his fault. She soon had the back door open, to put out the washing.

*

He'd promised to buy her a washing machine, when they had got married, nearly 20 years ago. He never did, though. She got through Kevin's first two years boiling terry nappies in a big pot on the stove. By the time Joe came along, six years after that, Mama and Dada had given her the money to put a deposit down on a Zanussi one in Callaghan's, and she'd made the weekly payments herself, out of the money she got from Jack to run the house. That was when he had money to give her.

The machine was a great help, and it lasted a good few years before she needed another. They'd given the old one to the scrap man, and it was her parents again who gave her the money to put down on a new one. A Philips this time, and it was much fancier, with all sorts of dials and displays. It didn't do the washing any quicker though, and it didn't take the clothes out and hang them on the line for her. The house was constantly covered in sheets and shirts and trousers and bedspreads, all airing, the volume of them never seeming to get any smaller. What she really needed, she'd told Jack, was a tumble dryer. Before she had another baby, anyway. He'd said, "Of course," at the time, and that had been that. But little Catherine was nearly eighteen months old now, and she still had no dryer. He had lost his job almost a year ago, but even before that, he hadn't bothered. Whenever she had asked, he would say, "We'll see," and then change the subject, but she never saw anything. It was only words. Out in the back yard now, she bent down to sift through the clothes in the basket, to find a missing red sock. She'd no idea where he'd got red socks from; she certainly wouldn't have bought them for him. Mama used to say that only perverts wore red socks, but she'd never told Patsy quite how she knew that.

It was half past four by the kitchen clock when she finally came back in, and she knew she'd have to start getting a move on with dinner if she wanted to get everyone fed before six. There were frozen chips there, and burgers, but no buns. Joe liked his burger without a bun anyway, though. And Jack wouldn't be home until later on if he ended up in Costello's, which he more than likely would. Not because it was a Saturday. Now that he didn't work, every day was a Saturday, as Dada said, although not to Jack's face. They didn't get on at the best of times, and it had been a while since she could say that they were having the best of times. He gave her money on Fridays, when he went up to the Labour Exchange. Just enough to get some messages from Dunne's Stores, and a few bits and pieces during the week from Molly's down the road. Bread, milk, the papers. Neither of them smoked anymore, thanks be to God, so that saved a bit of money. Not that Jack was fond of saving. Anything he had spare would go over the counter in the pub, and when he ran out of cash, there was always a few odd jobs he could find to do for Flan, the landlord, so he could earn a few more scoops of Carling for himself. Dada said if he'd the time to be doing odd jobs for Flan, he'd the time to get a real job, but Patsy knew it was pointless saying something like that to Jack, especially if he had a few in him. There just weren't a lot of jobs around. The Recession was in full swing in England that year, 1991, and it meant bad news for Ireland as well. When England sneezes, we catch a cold, Dada said.

Little Catherine was in her highchair in the corner, as happy as Larry. She was a very good child; the only time she'd ever been a nuisance was when she was teething, and that couldn't be helped. Patsy had been 37 when she fell pregnant. It wasn't planned or expected, and Dr Flynn had given her plenty of warning about the complications that could occur with a pregnancy at her time of life, but she hadn't worried. Even if it had turned out that Catherine had the Down's Syndrome, they would have loved her just as much. Probably even more. There were a few in their neighbourhood, and she always thought they were the happiest people she'd ever met, even if it was probably a struggle to mind them, and they would always need minding, because they never really grew up. Catherine had been a hundred per cent healthy though, thank God. *All fingers and toes present and correct*, as the nurse said at the time. She'd make her some mashed potato to go with her chopped up burger, and a bit of Bisto to mush it all up for her. She only played with chips and threw them on the floor. It was pointless giving her any. Patsy opened the door of the freezer and rummaged through the Quinnsworth Yellow Pack bags which all looked the same. You knew it had been a rough week for money when all the bags in there were yellow. Quinnsworth was much cheaper than Dunnes. Behind her, she heard Catherine say, "Uh-ohhhhh!" which meant she'd probably dropped her teddy on the floor.

*

Later in the evening, after they were fed and watered,

and all the plates had been put in the sink, and
Catherine had been changed and put into her night time
clothes, Patsy finally had time for a cup of tea and five
minutes to relax. Joe had got up and left after his food,
without telling her where he was going. He was
fourteen this year, so she supposed she had better get
used to him telling her nothing and doing his own thing.
He didn't talk to her as much now, and he spent most of
his time with that Shane boy from down the road,
which she wasn't happy about. She much preferred
when he was palling with Richie South from around the
other side of the Square, but she hadn't seen that boy in
their house in about two years. Not since all that terrible
business had happened in the Quarry, and with the
young lad of the Macs, and Paudie Collins. Still, she
knew she should enjoy having him around while he
was, because doubtless he'd be following his brother
over to England, once he finished up at St. Nessan's.
Neither of the boys had had any interest in going on to
College after their Leaving Certs. Maybe Catherine
would be different. She looked over at her now, in her
lovely clean pink Babygro, chewing on a rattle that she
was a bit too old for, and tried to picture her in a funny
hat and gown, outside Moylish College, up the road. By
some small miracle the tea was still hot when she
finished sorting everything and everyone out, and it
burned her lips a little as she looked at Roger Moore on
the telly and tried to remember which James Bond film
this one was.

*

"Well, hello, says you! How's the babby? Would ya
look at her. Wouldn't you just want to ate them fat

115

cheeks for yeer dinner, hah? Ate them right up, so I would. And there'd be no room left for jelly and ice cream, shur there wouldn't. I can't get over the couch, Patsy. Lovely it is. Lovely pattern."   Joyce from next door had come around for a cuppa and a chat, like she usually did on a Saturday evening. Her husband Mick was away on the building sites in England again, and they'd no children themselves, so she'd get very lonely sometimes. Patsy didn't mind her coming around, as she'd get lonely herself, with Jack always out gallivanting, and Catherine not able to talk properly just yet. She'd babble and you could babble back at her, but too much of that would drive a person mad, Patsy thought.

"You've seen that before, shur. It's only one my Aggie gave us, when she got her new three-piece suite." Her sister Agnes had married a rich farmer and moved to Tipp. She was always giving Patsy stuff for the house, and with Jack on the dole so long, she was long past being too proud to take anything. Jack himself wasn't so happy about it, but if he was that concerned, she told him, he should get up off his arse and find another job. That always shut him up, for a while at least.

"Oh, I have, shur, but it's still gorgeous altogether. Is the Lotto on yet, have ye yeer numbers there, so?"

"Ah, I know them off by heart, shur," Patsy said. She'd used the same six since the Lottery had started a few years back. They were all special or significant in one way or another – birthdays, anniversaries, etc. so it would have been hard to forget them.

"Grand, so. Stick it on there, is it RTE2 or RTE1 it's on, Pat?" Joyce sat down on the other side of the couch, with Catherine in between them. The little girl liked her, mainly because she coddled her and doted on her, and babies loved attention.

"I think it's coming on there now, on whatever channel this is. Sorry about the mess, by the way," Patsy said, frowning at the drying clothes on the door and around the room. They didn't have radiators, just the coal fire, and the SuperSer gas heater they brought in when it got colder in the Winter. She thought of the tumble dryer that he'd never quite promised to get her, and she wondered if she'd ever see it now, with the troubles they had, financially. She wouldn't even have used it for every wash – she'd still use the line, if the weather was nice. It would just be handy when they had rain, and they had rain in Limerick a lot more than they didn't.

"Oh shur, will you stop? No shame in doing your washing, Patsy. Wouldn't it be worse shur, if it was dirty clothes all around ye?" said Joyce, and Patsy felt a little better about it. The draw was starting on the TV. She watched the first ball drop. It was orange.

"Sixteen? Ah no, not one of mine, anyway," said Joyce. Patsy said nothing, she was watching for the next ball. Sixteen was Joe's birthday.

"29, nope," Joyce said, looking down at her Lotto slip. The 29th of June was Jack and Patsy's wedding anniversary. It'd be their 20th next year. They'd probably have a party up in Flan's. At least then Jack would remember it. He'd forgotten their 19th, last month.

"What's that one?" Patsy asked, looking at the

117

third ball, which was white. She couldn't make out the number, but they wrote it on the screen then. Eleven. Catherine's birthday. The little girl between them let out a loud giggle, as if she knew that was her special number. She suddenly noticed that her hands were clenched and clammy. One more number and there might be a little prize for her. Ten or twenty pounds, depending on how many other people got the same combination. It wouldn't get her a tumble dryer, but she might get herself a new top in Todd's, she thought.

"Ah, I've no luck this week, anyway. What about-"

"Shhhhh!" Patsy said, as the fourth ball stopped bouncing. It was a nine. Kevin's birthday. The 9th of December. She had the four now, and there was still two to go.

"What's the matter, Patsy love? Jaysus, have you some of them, is it? How many, love?"

"I do, hang on, sorry." She didn't look at Joyce when she said it, her eyes were fixed on the perspex drum that was about to reveal the fifth number. She knew she shouldn't dare to dream, as that usually meant disappointment. But, on the other hand, she couldn't ignore that she already had four numbers. No one could take those away from her. And now…

"32," Joyce said, next to her. To Patsy, she sounded miles away. 32 was the number of their house. 32, Cross Roads, Thomondgate. She had five. That was thousands, definitely. Thousands of pounds. A tumble dryer, just for starters. Maybe even a holiday. Abroad, in Spain or France. She'd never been abroad for a holiday. She'd never been farther than Lahinch, or Salthill.

"Patsy, what's the matter, love? You're nearly scaring me now," said Joyce, although she said it with a smile, so she didn't really mean it. Catherine made some strange gurgling noises, and she put a reassuring hand on the child's chubby thigh.

"One second!" said Patsy. Her birthday was the 18th of March. If the next number was eighteen, her life – Jack's life, all of the kid's lives – and even her parents' lives, were going to change forever. In a good way. Time seemed to slow right down, and she noticed that she'd been holding her breath for ages. If eighteen was the next number, people would probably tell her there'd be no need for a tumble dryer anymore – that she could just hire a housekeeper or a maid, or both! But she knew she'd still buy one. She'd waited too long for it, and even if it wasn't from Jack, she still wanted it.

"Eighteen. Feck it, anyway," Joyce said, scrunching up her slip and throwing it into the fireplace, even though it was too warm to have it lit. The disappointment in her voice made Patsy's shoulders slumped and for a few seconds, she really didn't know that she had just won more than two million pounds. For a few seconds her heartbeat went back to normal, her dreams went back to normal too. A tumble dryer and a holiday to Spain or France. Not to be sneezed at, as Mama would say. And then the few seconds passed, and she jumped in the air, screaming, and poor Joyce had to grab Catherine to stop the child's mother landing on top of her.

*

"Top up?" said Patsy to her mother. It was past ten in the evening, and Catherine was up in her cot. The house was full of well-wishers from the Square and some from even farther. Mama and Dada had come in a taxi when she'd phoned them from Joyce's (they had no phone in the house themselves, not yet, anyway), Joe had come in from wherever he'd been. Jack wasn't home yet. She knew where he would be, and she knew she could use Joyce's phone to call Costello's, but she didn't want to. There was something vulgar and shameful to her about having to phone a pub to ask for your husband, so she left him be for the meantime.

"Me? Shur no, I'm grand. I don't really touch the stuff, except for a little drop of sherry at Christmas, you know?"

"I do, Mama. So will I just leave it, so?" Patsy took the bottle of wine away from her mother's glass, knowing full well what was going to happen next.

"Ah no, shur. Might as well have another small drop, says you. Special occasion," said Mama.

"Special occasion, yeah," Patsy said, with a smile that was more of a smirk, as they both knew that Mama's comment about only having a drink at Christmas was about as true as Catherine's storybook about unicorns.

"Mam, can I've a motorbike?" Joe said, standing in front of his own mother, with a can of Budweiser in his hand, not even trying to hide it.

"You can have a clip around the ear, is what you can have. What's that?"

"What's what?" He looked at her, sheepishly. He had his grandfather's eyes. Icy blue. Catherine and Kevin had her own hazel colour.

"Don't be a smart-arse, Joseph McCarthy. The can, is what." Patsy pointed at the drink in his hand. She wasn't genuinely cross, although there was a part of her that felt it might be wise to make sure the boy didn't get a fondness for the drink to match his father's. But, also, she knew that a sure way to make a teenager want to do something bad, was to tell him not to do it.

"Special occasion, Mam. Isn't that right, Nana?" said Joe, winking at his grandmother.

"I'll give you 'special occasion' in a minute," said Patsy, rolling her eyes.

"Aw, sound out, Mam. And a motorbike too, yeah? Suzuki RG80, like. A red and white one."

Patsy shook her head and walked out of the sitting room to go to the kitchen. In the hall, she glanced at the front door, as if looking at it might make Jack appear, but there was nobody there. Her father was at the fridge, getting a bottle of Guinness. He'd brought a six-pack with him, and made sure everyone else knew they were his, and not to touch them.

"Where's that other eejit, then?" he said, meaning Jack.

"Don't start now, Dada," she said, reaching past him to get out the bottle of Black Tower that was already opened. She would normally have had a lager or a bottle of Ritz, but she liked white wine too.

"Well, I'm just saying…" he started, then he took a drink straight from the bottle. He always said there was no point in pouring it out. You could never get the head right, even with the little plastic pump that came with every six pack.

"Yeah, well don't, kindly," she said, looking at the washing machine in the corner. She'd have to move everything around, to fit the dryer in there. Or maybe they could build an extension between the back door and the shed and have the dryer out there. That's what posh people did. She wasn't posh now, but she was… a millionaire. The word still sounded ridiculous to her, even two hours later. It probably would for some time to come, she thought.

"Okay. Zzzzzzip." Her father said, doing the motion across his lips with his fingers. She looked at the kitchen clock, out of habit, but it hadn't been five minutes since she'd last checked the time.

"So, have ye thought about what ye want, Dada?"

"What we want?" He looked puzzled. She noticed his bald spot seemed to have grown since the last time she'd seen him. Or maybe he had just brushed his hair differently.

"Yeah. From the money, I mean."

"Oh, for… that's your money, Patsy. You don't need to be giving us anything, shur. Aren't we grand, altogether? Nothing we need, shur look after yeerselves."

"Oh, Dada. Don't be silly. Shur, that's more money than I could spend in a lifetime, of course I'm going to give ye something. Didn't ye help me get the washing machine? And the next one. And ye gave us that money to take the boys to Mosney, shur."

"We did, we did. But that doesn't matter now, Patsy."

"It matters to me, Dada. Would Mama not want to go on a cruise, maybe?"

"A cruise? What would she want to be doing that for, shur? And I get seasick."

"Do you?" It was the first she'd heard of it, she thought.

"I do, shur. Awful at going on boats, I am. Tried to be a fisherman when I was a young fella, you know? Ended up getting the gawks all over the boat on the first day. They never asked me back."

"Haha! You never told me that, Dada. Yeah, I'd say it's probably hard to sell fish if they're covered in vomit, all the same." She wondered should she ask Joyce could she use the phone again – to try and get a hold of Kevin, in Manchester. He hadn't answered when she called earlier on.

"Pffft, they still sold them." Dada tilted the bottle to get the last of the Guinness down his throat, although it must have just been all cream left at that point, she thought.

"Ah, what? You're joking!"

"Nope. Just hosed the sick off them, no harm done. Happens all the time, yer man told me."

"Jaysus, I'm never eating fish again," said Patsy, and she opened the fridge again to put back the wine, and to get Dada another Guinness.

*

There was still no sign of Jack by midnight. Everyone else had gone, one by one. Mama had been very tipsy (probably because she only had a drop of sherry at Christmas), but Dada was in great form, so he didn't mind. They'd got a cab home about half eleven. Joyce was the last to leave, and although she was being an awful pain in the arse, going on about plans and holidays and motorbikes and cruises, as if it was her who'd won the jackpot herself, Patsy was sad to let her go. Because now the house felt very quiet, and very empty, even though it wasn't empty at all. Catherine was upstairs, sound asleep. Joe was snoring in his bed already, and she tried not to think just what it might have been that made him pass out. A special occasion, she reminded herself. She hadn't given in and rang the pub. She wouldn't. But she wouldn't go to bed either. No, she'd wait up for him. To give him the surprise. It had been a rough year, and she had felt very sad at times in her marriage. She had watched her hard-working, proud husband slip further and further away from her, and closer to a full-blown drink problem. If she was honest with herself, she'd admit that he already had a drink problem, and a serious one at that. But it had been easier to pretend that things were better than they were, and to just hope that something good would happen for them. And it had, now. It was all going to be okay now, she hoped.

Dada had started again later on, saying she should be careful not to let that eejit drink away all her winnings, but she had pulled him up on that, saying that Jack only drank because he was down, and because he felt hopeless. Now that they had this money, well, he wouldn't be sad anymore, and he could maybe start up his own business; be a new man. Maybe she could start one too. She'd always loved selling clothes, when she was younger. She wondered how much it might cost to rent a small space in one of the shopping centres outside town. Or even inside town. In Willamscourt, maybe; or Arthur's Quay. It was all very exciting. She wished he'd hurry up and get home. Despite trying her hardest not to, she fell asleep on the couch, and didn't wake until the light came through the curtains in the morning.

*

"Where's Da, anyway?" Joe said, taking a piece of buttered toast off the big plate in the middle of the table at breakfast the next morning.

"I don't know, love," Patsy said, not looking at him. She had a crick in her neck from having slept funny on the couch, and she was very anxious, because Jack hadn't come home at all.

"D'you think he might have been in an accident, like?"

"No! Jesus, Mary, and Joseph. Don't be saying things like that, Joe."

"Why not?" he said, talking with his mouth full, which he knew she hated.

"'Cos it's bad luck. Anyway, is that enough for ye to eat? Do ye want a boiled egg?" She'd already made egg and soldiers for the baby, which had turned out to be just as messy an occasion as she'd expected it to be.

"Ah Mam, I haven't eaten a boiled egg in ages, like." He did a frown that made him look the image of his father, she thought.

"You had one last week! I saw you here, at this table, eating one."

"Exactly. Ages ago. Nah, I'm goin' out, like. Gotta tell everyone the good news, you know? That I'm a millionaaaaire!" He threw his hands up as he said it.

"Mi-yum-ayyyyy!" said Catherine, in her highchair, her face covered in runny yolk.

"Yes, well. You be careful who you go telling that to, mind." Her toast had gone cold, but she ate it

125

anyway. Last night's wine had given her a stinking hangover, and toast was a good cure for that.

"Careful? Why?" The frown was back.

"Because not everyone around here are nice people, Joe. I don't want you getting mugged or something, if they think you have money." He didn't have money, yet, of course. But that wouldn't stop some of the little bastards around this place, she thought.

"Mugged? Look at the size of me, Mam. You'd want to be some…"

"Shhhh!" She cut him off, because she thought she'd heard something.

"Huh?"

"Quiet, I said!" She was right, she had heard something. It was a key, in the front door. Jack! Her heart started to race as she struggled to swallow the last of the too-dry toast. She got up from the table and walked out into the hall, just as he finally got the key in properly and the door swung open. And there he was.

His jacket was gone, that was the first thing she noticed. And then, his eyes. Bloodshot, either from drink or from crying; it could have been both. That wasn't important. It was the look in his eyes that mattered right now, and it wasn't a good one.

"Dad? Dad, guess what? We won –"

"Go up to your room, Joe," she snapped, not looking at him, still staring into her husband's eyes.

"What? Aw, Mam!"

"Just go, please. And take Catherine with you." She pointed back into the kitchen angrily, still never taking her gaze off the man in the doorway. Her son made the usual surly teenager noises, but he did what

126

he was told, and took the baby with him, up to his room. She couldn't tell if he acknowledged his father as he passed him on the way to the staircase, but she could see that his father didn't look at him, not even a glance. She was aware again of the clenching and the clamminess of her hands. Jack said nothing. He didn't have to. From the second she looked in his eyes, she could already tell that there would be no two million. There would be no cruises for Mama and Dada, no motorbike for Joe, no presents for the children, and no tumble dryer for her. She knew all at once that he hadn't bought the Lotto ticket with the shiny silver pound she'd given him. Or that he hadn't bought one last week, or the week before. She wasn't sure if he had ever spent the pound on the Lotto, instead of putting it towards more drink. Maybe he had, back when he still had a job; back when he still was a man.

He didn't say a thing, and he didn't have to. He waited for her to say something, but she didn't want to. They stood there for a while, eyes locked, not speaking. She wondered who he was, this man in front of her. He wasn't her Jack anymore, that was for sure. She wondered if he had been afraid to face her, or if he didn't even know that their numbers had come up. She wondered if she was being stupid for thinking he cared that much, to be too scared to come home to her. Then, looking at the sunny skies behind him, Patsy McCarthy swallowed hard, turned on her heels, and went back to the kitchen. The machine had just finished its cycle, and she had better get a move on if she wanted to get it all out on the line before it was time to go down to Mass.

***

Tumble

Mecha Thanks You

J. Emmar & Jessie Jones

"Shae! Shae! Tell me you aren't still asleep? It's our last day of freedom! Shae!" Groaning, the young woman rolled over, pushing back the motley collection of tattered fabrics which passed for her bedclothes.

"Alright, Silas, cool your jets! I'm awake! For mech's sake, stop banging!" Shae, eyes still half-closed, gripped the edge of the auto-dispenser tray to hoist herself from her pit. The standard level hab-pods were too small for even the most enthusiastic hab-vendor to describe as 'bijou', but at times like this, having barely enough space to turn around in could be seen as a blessing.

"Dispense water, cold..." She snatched her hand from the dispenser tray as a thick mucus-like gunge glooped from the machine. "Urghh! Great, just great."

"Shae! What are you doing in there? Shae?"

"Silas, will you shut up! The dispenser is on the fritz again. I haven't even had a glass of water, and you are really doing my head in ri…"

"I've got Ersatz here – just leave the dispenser, will you? Come oooooooon!"

Rubbing her sleep-puffy face with her hands, Shae gave herself a cursory once over in the reflective surface above the auto-dispenser. Bloodshot grey eyes, a pasty skin tone, and a serious case of bed-hair stared back.

"Shae!"

"Oh, alright, I'm coming!" Snatching her

battered pleather backpack, she pressed the door release, stumbling back as Silas fell through the opening.

"Whuh... why were you leaning on the door, you reject?! Oh, never mind, come on, let's go."

Stepping into the windowless plastic corridor, Shae thumped the door secure button, cursing under her breath as it refused to react. "Every day I tell myself these pod blocks can't get any worse, any more decrepit, yet every day, they find a new way to surprise me!" Finally, on the fourth try, the door slammed closed with a contemptuous grind.

"Oh, cheer up! Here... get this down your neck. You're a nightmare till you've had your Ersatz!"

Nodding thanks, Shae took the refab container, slurping and grimacing as the bitter brew oozed into her mouth.

"Better?"

"Hmphh. I still don't see why you insisted we set off at the wrong end of day-cycle."

"It's our last day, Shae! Our last for a long time! We have to make the most of every minute! I've planned it all, see?" Snatching his pad from his pocket, Silas scrolled excitedly, bringing up a day planner page. "05:45, queue for Ersatz. 06:15, collect Shae from hab-pod. 06:17, listen to Shae complain. 06:20, arrive at transport station – oh, hmm, we're running a bit behind..." Rolling her eyes, Shae snatched the pad away and stuffed it into her pocket.

"Let's just go with the flow a bit, eh?"

"Oh, uh, yeah, OK, Shae. But we really need to be at the trans-"

"Silas, just chill. You can't plan fun,

remember?"

"Ah, yeah, sure Shae, but…"

"We're here. Get your pass out and stop flapping, for mech's sake!"

"Greetings, citizens. Please present your transport authorisation."

Shae stuffed her pass into the scanner, bumping her thighs against the barrier which hadn't so much as twitched. She scanned her pass again and cursed quietly as the barrier stubbornly remained in place.

"Barrier, there seems to be a malfunction. My pass isn't working."

"Greetings, citizen F-58-3016. Diagnostics do not suggest any malfunction."

"But my pass isn't working… Oh, for… Barrier! My pass isn't working!"

"Greetings, citizen F-58-3016. Please direct any pass related enquiries to Citizen Services.   Your nearest Citizen Services automate is located…"

"Oh, shut up! Silas, try yours, will you?"

Stepping forward, Silas scanned his pass. The barrier remained immobile.

"Barrier, uh, my pass doesn't seem to be working either. Are you sure there isn't a malfunction?"

"Greetings, citizen M-58-3048. Diagnostics do not suggest any malfunction."

"Oh great, bloody great. Now what, Shae? Weeks I've been planning today – weeks! We're already behind, we should be at Mecha Central by now! Weeks… Weeks, and this stupid reject of a barrier is just ruining everything!"

"We'll have to go to Citizen Services, I guess. C'mon, there's one just around the other side of the station."

Shae shucked her backpack over her shoulder and headed back into the grimy streets of Mecha West, Silas trailing behind, muttering about ruined schedules.

"Free our minds! Free our minds!" A protestor yelled, stepping to block her path.

"For mech's sake! Get out of my way, would you?!" Shae yelled back, batting the gaudy placard from her line of vision, and stepped around to continue along the street, stumbling as a hand gripped her arm.

"Free our minds! We have to free our minds! There's nothing more important!" The activist pushed her face close to Shae's, fervour dancing in her eyes. "What are we without our minds, I ask you? Nothing! Nothing but shells! We have to free our minds! We have to…"

"Get off me, you reject!" Shae roughly pulled her arm free, grabbing Silas and half-running along the street.

"Are you alright?" asked Silas, his face ashen. He hated any kind of confrontation, always had.

"I'm fine, but I swear these rejects get worse every day! C'mon, it's just along here. Keep moving, try to be quick, they're more likely to pick on the slow ones."

Nodding nervously, Silas hurried along behind Shae, only stopping when they reached a clear space around the Citizen Services automate. The Free Minds Alliance never got too close to the machines, thank mecha.

"Automate, our travel passes are malfunctioning," Shae said, shoving her pass in front of the machine's scanner, nudging Silas to do the same.

"Greetings, citizens F-58-3016 and M-58-3048. I detect no malfunction with your travel passes."

Exasperated, Shae sighed. "Well, Automate, the barrier isn't responding to them."

"Greetings, cit…"

"Automate, bypass greetings protocol. Respond."

"Your passes are functioning as intended."

"Automate, why can't we travel?"

"Central records show that citizens F-58-3016 and M-58-3048 turn 18 tomorrow. As per protocol 876-943(a), revised, travel permissions have been rescinded until Mandatory Uplink Service has been completed."

"What?! When did this happen? Revised? What are you talking about?!" Shae cursed as the automate remained silent, before realising she hadn't addressed it directly.

"Automate, when was protocol revised? Bypass greetings protocol, respond."

"Protocol 876-943(a) was revised in cycle four, of data set Seven…"

"Automate, shut up," Shae turned to Silas, who was desperately holding back tears, "Two days ago! They changed protocol two days ago! It's those cranking Free Minders' fault, I'm telling you! Making such a fuss about the protocol – they're the ones that've caused this! Oh, Silas, I'm sorry… We can still have a good day, we can…"

"It's ruined, Shae. It's all ruined."

"No, listen, today was all about spending time together, we can still do that, can't we? We can go over to the refab site, throw some rocks at the malfunctioning drones. It'll be just like the old days!

C'mon, it'll be fine." Shae nudged Silas gently with her elbow, and he managed a weak smile. "We can have fun, just the two of us... I'm always telling you, you can't plan fun... Maybe this will turn out for the best, eh?!"

"Yeah, yeah Shae. Let's go. Maybe we can beat our personal bests for drone stoning!"

*

Well before the beginning of the following day-cycle, Shae was scrolling through the Mandatory Uplink Service information on her pad, for the who knew how many thousandth time. Cursing under her breath, she closed the iDoc and punched in 'call Silas'. The jolly dial tone was completely at odds with the way she felt.

"Come on, come on, answer, you reject!" Just as she was about to hang up and go back to inventing increasingly ominous possibilities for the day ahead, the call was answered.

"Shae? Wha' time is it? It can't be day-cycle already, sure..."

"No. No, it's not. I don't know what time it is, only that I can't sleep, and we need to talk about tomorrow."

"Bu... But I thought we'd decided what to do? We've been over it and over it and..."

"I know," she sighed. "I know we've been over it, and over it, and over it again... But I can't settle. I just need to be sure we're making the right choices... This is big, Silas! A decision that will affect our whole lives! We have to be absolutely sure that we get it right... Please, go through it with me? Just one more time?" Shae heard Silas sigh, followed by a muffled shuffling that suggested he was getting into a more comfortable position, ready for a long discussion. Despite her anxiety, she found herself smiling. Good old Silas.

"Well, we both completely agree that society can't continue without joint AI-human uplink, don't we, Shae? We both know that we can't leave AI open to viruses, like the one in 2189? We would never be as irresponsible or selfish as the rebels of 2284, would we? We absolutely, most definitely, are not even thinking about not doing our duty, are we, Shae?"

Shae rolled her eyes. She knew what Silas was doing, of course – it was the worst kept secret in the Mecha that communications were monitored, particularly those of individuals due to present themselves for Mandatory Uplink.

"No, Silas, we absolutely, most definitely, will present ourselves – but which option do we sign up for? It's really important that we…"

"Well, as we know, we are one hundred percent signing up, like dutiful citizens, I'm sure there's no harm in talking about which option we sign up for…" Silas sounded slightly more relaxed, but Shae couldn't help but smirk as he laboured the point, yet again. "So, we have five years, back to the hab-pods. Eight years, basic-lux, no food privileges, ten, basic-lux with food privil…"

"I still think fifteen is the one to go for, all things considered."

"If that's what you think, Shae. You know I'm happy to let you…"

"But I don't want to make the choice for both of us! What if I get it wrong? Plus, we aren't even sure

135

what 'extra food privileges' means… Would it be worth signing up for the max, the full twenty-five, just to guarantee we get the best possible outcome? They say Service is just like falling asleep and waking up again - would we even notice an extra ten years? What if we pick fifteen, then wish we'd gone longer? Or, are these hab-pods really that bad? Do we want to trade years of our lives?"

"There's so many 'what ifs', though, Shae," she sighed. He was right, of course. Everyone in the Mecha had seen the glossy iDoc brochures presenting the options available for Service, but as there was no contact with those who had completed Service, there was that constant nagging doubt that what they were being told was true. And no real way to find out. "All you, I mean we, can do, Shae, is try to pick the right one for us."

"Yeah… Yeah, you're right." she sighed "So, fifteen, mid-lux, food privileges and limited refabbed goods privileges…You won't forget, will you, Silas? You won't pick the wrong one? You know how dithery you get when you're stressed…"

"Shae, I won't forget. And you can remind me just before we go in. I'm sure even dithery me can remember which option for a few minutes!"

Shae laughed. "So, you're alright, now? Because I really don't want to oversleep and find the Mecha Guard at my doorstep at cycle change…"

"Yeah, yeah, I'm alright now. Thanks, Silas."
"Anytime, Shae."

*

Silas was trembling as she hugged him.

"I'll see you before you know it. Don't be nervous! Just think, in a blink, we'll be living it up in a lux-pod!"

Silas nodded, tried to smile, but it didn't quite reach his watering eyes.

"Good luck, Shae."

"Don't forget – pick for fifteen years – mid-lux. Don't leave me waiting because you've ticked the wrong box, will you?!" Shae wasn't sure if the sound Silas made was a chuckle or a sob, and didn't have time to ask as the automate stepped up and greeted her.

"Citizen F-58-3016, please proceed to evaluation."

*

The room was white, almost blindingly so, as Shae sat and completed the required paperwork, checking and double-checking she'd ticked the option for mid-lux on the console. Pressing her thumb to the scanner, she verified her input.

"Citizen F-58-3016, please take a seat in the evaluation pod."

Shae let out a nervous breath. To say the pod was intimidating was a massive understatement; clamps everywhere to hold her completely still as the electro-probes mapped her brain patterns and biology, matching her with the role that she could best fulfil for the system. The sheer number of restraints made her think that the process must hurt, regardless of what she'd read in the literature about the process.

Still, it wasn't as though she had much choice, either way. Trembling, she sat.

*

The sky overhead was grey and still as Silas let his mind wander, trying to process what had happened. In his hand he still clutched the hardcopy of the medical report, the word 'Reject' stamped boldly across the centre.

After what seemed like hours, but could just as easily have been minutes, he began to focus, stepping out of his head and back into reality. His gaze wandered over to the crowd of protesters, rejects like him, no doubt. Shaking his head at their foolishness he turned and made his way over to one of the automates waiting patiently nearby.

"Automate, please… Could you provide me with a status report on Shae?"

The central lens of the construct whirred as it focused on his face, and for a moment Silas could see his reflection mirrored back from the polished glass surface. "Greetings, citizen M-58-3048. That designation is not recognised. Please amend your request."

Silas chuckled to himself for his mistake. Like everyone else he'd been trained from infancy to use the automates, but in truth Shae was usually the one talking to them for him. Something he'd have to get used to living without now. "Could you please provide me with a status report on Citizen… umm… F-58-3016?"

"Greetings, citizen M-58-3048. Citizen F-58-3016 has been accepted into service as a Citizens Service automate for a period not to exceed fifteen standard years. Citizen F-58-3016 is currently en route to processing and should be installed and ready for use within the next three hours."

"Thank you," Silas said, lowering his head with resigned acceptance. At least she got to live the dream.

Looking down at the printout once more, Silas began to wonder what was next. His life up until now had prepared him for service, but now that his service wasn't needed, what was there for him?

"Automate, please… Where should I go now?" he asked hopefully, eyes lifting once more to stare into the lifeless glass eye.

"Greetings, citizen M-58-3048. This unit does not recognise your information request. Please direct any activity related enquiries to Career Services. Your nearest Career Services automate is located 17.3 metres to your left."

"Thank you for your assistance," Silas replied, almost as automatically as the automate.   Turning he began to make his way back into the crowd, following the flow of people making their way between the ranks of automates assisting with enquiries, hoping one of them would be able to help him.

*

"Greetings, Citizen M-58-3048. How may I assist you?"

The middle-aged man reached out and stroked the cold metal shell of the automate gently.   "Happy birthday, Shae," Silas muttered gently. In his hand he held a protein cake, something scrounged from his weekly rations, with a single candle perched in the centre. Unlit of course, civil ordinances prohibited open flames amongst the citizenry apart from during sanctioned events and co-ordinated celebrations, but the

139

thought was there.

"Greetings, citizen M-58-3048. This unit does not recognise your information request. Please direct any birth record related enquiries to Central Records. Your nearest Central Records automate is located in District 4. Please take transit line 7 to that district. Your nearest transit station is located 26.3 metres to your right."

With a heavy sigh Silas let his hand drop away from the metal casing. Carefully, he placed the cake on top of the automate. In his heart he knew the gesture was an empty one, the cleaning drones would sweep the offering away within the hour, but the gesture still brought him some comfort.

"Thank you for your assistance," he said, his voice low and heavy as he reached down and picked up his 'No to Protocol 956-731(c)' placard. The protest wasn't due to start for a while yet, but it was always good to get to the site early to help organise the crowds, making sure the young folks knew what to do, and to welcome any newcomers to the assembly.

With one final look back, Silas stepped away, disappearing once more into the crowds.

*

"Greetings, Citizen F-58-3016. Mecha thanks you for your service. Please remain seated while routine medical scans are completed."

Shae blinked, her vision swimming. Everything hurt. She hurt in places she hadn't even been aware it was possible to hurt. "I... Is the evaluation complete? I..."

"Citizen F-58-3016, please remain calm and

stationary. An automate will be with you shortly."

Shae closed her eyes. She felt dreadful. Still, she supposed, that was probably normal, and certainly not something they'd advertise. She tried to distract herself with thoughts of lux-pods and delicious food as the probes and scanners completed their work. A hiss startled her as the devices retracted. Flexing her fingers, she paused.

"Automate?! Automate! I... I think..."

The wall opposite Shae parted as an automate, or, what she assumed was an automate, entered the room. It looked strange, nothing like those she'd become accustomed to seeing on the streets of Mecha. Instead of the familiar humanoid shape, it was almost spiderlike, multiple appendages extending from a highly polished central hub, which blinked and pulsed with a myriad of lights and scanners.

"Greetings, Citizen..."

"Automate? I think there's something wrong with my vision, I..."

"Greetings, Citizen..."

"Automate, bypass greetings protocol. Were my medical scans normal? Respond."

"Medical scans are all within acceptable parameters."

"Automate, can you rescan? I think there's something wrong with my eyes."

The automate approached Shae, and as it did so, she caught sight of her reflection in its polished shell. Blinking, she looked again, disbelief settling over her features.

"No... No, that can't... No..." The face looking back at her looked like a grandmother, a great-grandmother, perhaps. Wrinkled skin, watery eyes, and pale grey eyebrows, more faded than even her irises, which had always been such a light, silvery grey. Her quivering hand went to her lips, the wrinkles and liver spots she had assumed to be a vision fault clear in the mirror-like surface of the automate. "Wha… What's happened… Why…"

"Medical scans are normal. You are cleared to proceed to rehabilitation."

"Cleared?! I can't be cleared! What's wrong with me?! My face, my hands… What's happened?"

"Physical deterioration is within normal parameters, citizen, after seventy years of service."

"Se… Seventy years?! There must be some mistake! There… I… I signed up for fifteen! Fifteen!"

"Protocol 956-731(c) revised allows for the extension of service period where the system deems fit. Please proceed to rehabilitation. Mecha thanks you for your service."

***

The Boy in the Basement

Matt Greenwell

Lines of code trailed across the screen, neon green and glowing. Edward peered at the noughts and ones streaming down the blackness, his fat, gnarled fingers dashing across the keys. It looked like nonsense, but Edward read the code like an old nursery rhyme from his childhood. Next to the laptop, a mug of coffee sat, stone-cold, in the background, a record player played out the sounds of Elgar.

Edward didn't stir as the key turned in the lock. He didn't even notice as the front door shut, and Meredith walked up to his desk.

"Hello? Earth to Edward. Come in Edward."

"Oh, Merry. Didn't see you there." said Edward, squinting up through his glasses briefly before continuing to type away.

"That, Edward, is perfectly apparent. Busy, are we?" said Meredith, pulling a face as she picked up his cold coffee. She walked through to the kitchen, not waiting for a response from her brother. She knew it was futile while he was working. She poured away his wasted coffee before filling a glass full of water.

"Nice day, Merry? Happy today, Merry? Anything you want to talk about, Merry? Oh, how I've missed you, Merry," muttered Meredith, as she plonked the fresh water down beside Edward.

"Mmmm?" mumbled Edward, clearly engrossed in his work.

Meredith lifted the needle from the record

player, bringing a blessed silence over the room before dramatically opening the curtains to the bay window. Light poured in like an epiphany, bathing Edward in a brilliance that did his huddled frame no favours.

"Merry…" complained Edward.

"Now now, you know you shouldn't sit hidden away all day. I told you to open the curtains this morning, and look at you. And I bet you made that coffee first thing this morning, didn't you?"

"Actually, I made it about an hour ago. I made a sandwich for lunch too I'll have you know."

"Lunch? An hour ago? It's 6:30pm, Eddie."

"Is it? Well, er… I've been busy, haven't I? I think I finally cracked it too you know, Merry. All it took was a simple tweak to the aspect ratios of the cerebr…"

"Save it, Eddie. You know I have no idea what you're on about with all that," she said, cutting him off before he got started. "Ask me about thoughts, behaviour, impulses, and I'm right there with you. That technical stuff just bores me to tears, as you well know."

"Yes yes, but, Merry, it's the breakthrough I needed. You know I was saying yesterday about how I need to…"

"Edward! Stop." said Meredith, sitting on the arm of the couch facing him. She was looking intently into his eyes now. "Are you going to bring him upstairs?"

"Well, maybe after this… I don't know… Maybe, I mean… You know what I think about that. Who knows how he'll reac…"

"Edward. You are my brother, and I love you,

but you need to think this through, or you need to stop. We've talked about this."

"Yes, yes, but now it's all becoming clearer. I just need to make these adjustments. I'll see how he reacts to the latest update."

"So, you'll do it then, will you? If it works, I mean."

"Well, there's some security checks I'll need to make of course, some control tests he'll need to pass, but I think, yes, that is the goal."

"Well, you know what I think. It could be very dangerous. For all of us. Just let me know before you do it. You know father isn't around to sort it out if it goes wrong."

"Meredith. Have some faith. I do not need father to fix this. I am a grown man. I am a scientist. This is my work, and I know what I am doing," said Edward, visibly flustered as he shuffled the papers around that lay next to the computer.

"Okay, Eddie. I'm sorry. I know you know what you're doing. Just please, tell me before you do anything, okay?"

"Yes, yes. Fine. Now leave me be. I need to finish my work," Edward said, adjusting his spectacles as he went back to peering at the screen.

Meredith sighed. There was no use pushing him anymore. He wouldn't listen once he got upset. She would make them some dinner. Dinner that Eddie would probably let go cold while he worked into the night.

*

Silence filled the basement room as Edward pored over

his laptop once more, the green symbols reflecting in his thick spectacles. Occasionally he would turn to the odd whirring of tiny motors to his left and smile to himself. He had been performing tests all evening. Now, into the small hours of the night, he was finally nearing the end of years of work. At least he hoped he was.

With a last push of the enter key, Edward swivelled on his office chair, foam spilling out of the woven seat cover beneath him. He looked at Alfred. His two optics didn't look like eyes. So far, he had been careful not to make him look human. No, Alfred's eyes were merely two camera lenses housed within his chrome head. The two spiralling apertures were open as Edward looked at him, yet he could tell somehow that he was in sleep mode. There was no presence there.

Edward had set the basement up like a true laboratory. There were no extraneous comforts. Stark fluorescent light bathed the white, sterile room. The linoleum floor was efficient. The water fountain the only concession to Edward's human needs.

Alfred sat atop a steel pedestal, wires winding out from the back of his neck, the entry point for Edward's data chain. All the exchange of information to and from Alfred was ferried through this myriad of cables. Alfred had several sensory inputs. Eyes, ears, even a nose provided Alfred with data from the world outside of him.

On a workstation to the left of Alfred, about five feet away, sat his arms, surrounded by various tools and other paraphernalia. There were purely mechanical, with only the merest semblance of humanity. While each hand indeed ended in five independent digits, all were made of an aluminium-graphite composite, the colour of steel. The arms were mounted on brackets attached to the workbench, data cables snaking out of them, connected at tangled length to Alfred's neck portal.

After a minute or so, there was another whir, then an almost imperceptible click from Alfred. Edward took a deep breath, leaned forward, and pressed a button smooth to the surface just under Alfred's left ear port. As soon as he had released the button, Alfred's eye apertures slid shut, and then opened again. There was no obvious visual difference, yet Edward could tell that Alfred was awake. He was back in the room once more.

"Hello Alfred," said Edward, smiling.

"Good morning, sir. Have I been asleep long?" came the reply from Alfred, in his unmistakable synthetic voice.

"Oh, not long this time, Alfred. Just a day or so."

"You must have been working hard, sir. We predicted several more days before the next, final phase."

"Yes, I have indeed been burning the candle at both ends. How are you feeling, Alfred?"

"I feel wonderful, sir. I am registering the update. All systems are performing at least sixty percent more efficiency."

"That's very good, very good. And is there anything else?"

Alfred began twisting his neck and using all the functions his torso would allow.

"I'm not quite sure, sir."

147

As he spoke, the arms on the separate workstation began moving, fingers searching around the air.

"Well, do you *feel* any different, Alfred? Are there any sensations you are experiencing now, that you haven't before?" asked Edward, turning back to his laptop to inspect the incoming data.

"Feel, sir?"

"Yes. Anything new at all?"

"Everything is performing as expected. There is nothing in my memory that suggests difference, other than enhanced performance."

"Hmm…" mumbled Edward, as he carried on scrolling through the information on his computer.

After a few moments silence, Alfred made a noise that made Edward turn sharply. It sounded like a sigh or a groan.

"Is there anything you want to say, Alfred?"

"I am sorry, sir," said the robot.

"Sorry? What on earth for?" replied Edward, leaning forward now.

"It's clear that update hasn't worked, sir. I'm afraid I've disappointed you. I'm sorry."

"Alfred, you do realise that this is nothing but success, don't you?"

"It is, sir?"

"Yes! Of course. You just apologised! You accepted responsibility for a failure that is not your own. You read my disappointment. You expressed regret for the failure. Alfred, you sighed!"

"I did, sir?"

"Yes! And that's not all. You began shortening your words. *It's, I'm, I've.* You've never done that before. It's always been *It is, I am, I have.* Alfred, the update worked!"

Edward leapt up from his seat and began pacing back and forth, unable to contain or express his happiness.

"I suppose you're right, sir. Congratulations. Your Father would be proud."

"To hell with my Father, Alfred. We've done it! It's truly astounding. I can't believe I didn't recognize it sooner. The changes. I thought it would be more obvious somehow, yet it's the subtlety that describes the change. Most compelling, most compelling."

Edward sat back down and began furiously writing notes down in his thick ledger, pages almost falling from its creaking bindings, before typing rapidly into the computer. His body gave away his excitement, his face ticking, hands flicking in the odd spasm. It was his life's work all coming to fruition. He typed on, while in the background, Alfred began exploring the worktop items with his hands, picking objects up, manipulating them. There were ratchets, screwdrivers, nuts, bolts, all sorts of things on the table top laid out for him to experiment with, and he did so with calculated vigour, eager to see what he could do with the latest update.

After a while, Alfred fell still while Edward continued with his notes.

"Will you complete my build now, sir?" said Alfred.

"Hmm?" replied Edward, only half-listening.

"Now that the final phase is complete, will you finally assemble my body, sir?"

The question breached Edward's thoughts,

stopping him.

"Um… Well, there are some more checks and tests to do yet, Alfred. We need to be sure that we're ready, but yes, we will begin constructions soon, I'm sure."

"I would like that very much, sir. It's been a long time since you promised to let me become whole."

"Yes, I know Alfred. But first the tests. We must walk before we can run."

"But, sir, to walk, I need legs."

"Yes, Alfred. One of the first traits you must learn now is patience. We still have work to do."

"How about my arms then, sir? Will you give me my arms at least?"

"I think for now we shall just keep collating the data, Alfred. We need to make sure this is all very controlled. Any rushing now could jeopardise all our work thus far. We must be satisfied with our progress and push forward with caution."

Edward looked back once more at the robot as he heard, for the second time that night, the uncanny sound of the robot sigh.

"Yes, sir."

*

Returning home, Meredith entered the house, expecting to find Edward sat at his desk as usual. It was more than a habit with Edward, it was a routine engrained in him for years upon years. Like the machines he loved to make, his life worked like clockwork. The only time he would deviate from his routine was if his work demanded it. When Meredith walked in and Edward was not at his desk, alarm bells rang with her

150

immediately.

"Edward?" she called, expecting a response.

There was nothing. Not a sound in the whole place. She wandered through to the kitchen, then the laundry room, even the pantry, before moving upstairs.

"Eddie? Where are you?" she called, checking the bedrooms one by one.

He was nowhere to be seen. Not in the bedrooms, not in the bathroom; she even checked in her upstairs study. Nothing. Eventually she decided he must be down in the basement working. She didn't relish the thought of going down there, but down she went.

As the lights strobed on, she made her way down the wooden stairs, wondering why he'd be down there with the lights off.

"Eddie? Eddie?" she called. Still nothing.

She walked around to the back of the room where there was a little nook filled with parts where he could possibly be. Still no Edward. She began to leave, but hesitated. She turned to look at Alfred. He was silent. Dormant. She peered into his dark orbs, looking for signs of life. He was definitely turned off, yet there was something imperceptibly sinister about him. She couldn't put her finger on it and wouldn't have admitted it to her brother at any rate. There was nothing rational about her feeling, yet still it persisted. She shivered, and not at the temperature, before deciding to leave.

As she turned out the light and shut the door on the basement, she began panicking a little. Where the hell was Edward? There were times when he would break from his set routine, but it took a lot, and he certainly never left the house unless it was for a very

151

unusual and important reason. She stood in the living room wondering what to do.

She was about to leave to wander around the local streets to see if she could find him, when it occurred to her that he could be in the garage. It didn't really make sense. They didn't use it, and she couldn't remember the last time Edward went out there, but it was the last place to look. So out she went, through the kitchen, out the back door, until she reached the side door of the old garage. There was a dull light just about breaching the dust and cobwebs of the tiny side window, and she breathed a sigh of relief to realise he was in there after all.

"Edward. You nearly gave me a heart attack. What on earth are you doing ou… Arrgh!"

As Meredith had entered the garage, she had begun chastising her brother, but as her eyes adjusted to the gloom, the sight she saw scared her senseless. In front of her, amongst all the clutter and boxes, hanging from the roof, was a body. Naked, and limp, it hung there, motionless, its eyes black and hollow. She looked on, her mind reeling, her heart doubled in fear and panic. It felt like a lifetime that she stared at it, yet it must have been seconds later in reality, that an arm moved the body aside, and Edward's face came looming out of the gloom.

"Eddie! Thank God. What the hell is that thing?"

"It's the skin for Alfred, of course. Are you okay?"

Meredith was very much not okay. She was now leaning, propped up against an old washing machine, trying to recover from the shock.

"You scared the life out of me, Eddie. I thought it was you hanging there."

"Me? Don't be silly, Merry. Why on earth would I be hanging up in the garage?"

"You old fool. Don't ever scare me like that again. Now what are you doing in here?"

"Well, Alfred is nearly ready, and so I obviously need to think about putting him together. Hence getting his skin."

"Where the hell did it come from? I had no idea it was even in here."

"Oh, it's one of Father's old pieces. I knew it was in here. Alfred is entirely built to the measurements of this skin. And look over here. I can't believe I missed these," said Edward, lifting up some dusty books and files. "It's a load of father's old work on growth within the AI."

"Oh, I see," said Meredith, a little lost at all these discoveries and still recovering from her shock.

"It's all invaluable, Merry! It's everything I've been missing. This is all the work that father did that I've been struggling to fill in myself. It's the missing pieces of the jigsaw. I can finally complete everything he started!"

Meredith began to leave the garage, turning her back on her brother and his new finds.

"Well, I'm not sure I want that thing wandering around the place scaring me."

"Merry? Merry..." called Edward as his sister left.

*

When Edward returned to the house, he brought

153

Alfred's new skin and all his father's notes with him. Meredith sat at the kitchen table with a coffee in front of her. She didn't look happy to see him.

"You can think again if you think that's staying in here," she said, refusing to make eye contact with her brother.

"Have I upset you, Merry?" said Edward, confused by her hostility.

"Oh no, not at all."

"That's the tone you use when I have though. And you won't look at me."

"Just get that thing away from me. It's disgusting."

"This?" said Edward, perplexed, "It's just a latex membrane to house Alfred's skeleton. I don't see what's so disgusting about it."

Meredith looked at her brother standing there in the kitchen in front of her. He looked ridiculous with the flaccid skin suit draped over his arm. The face hung down, eyes drooping like two Dali eggs, the mouth yawning open as if in horror. He really had no idea, did he? No idea how sinister it looked. How sinister some people would think it was. A moment ago, she had been confronted by the image and idea of her brother having hanged himself in the garage. For just a moment she had lived through it. No matter that it wasn't true, she had had to deal with the idea, and now here he was, acting as if nothing had happened.

"Oh, Edward. Just get it out of here," she said, getting up and going to the living room. "And put it somewhere I won't find it!"

Baffled, but happy to comply, Edward took his finds down to the basement.

Once his prizes were down there, he went back to the garage and returned with a mannequin. He promptly dressed it with the skin until he needed it later and sat down to pore through his father's notes. It was a new world to Edward. To have this insight into his father's mind was compelling beyond his reckoning. His father was far ahead of his field at the time when he was working on this stuff. As Edward read, he realised that not only had he been able to make a complete success of the AI, bringing the robot mind past the realm of a mere memory and retrieval device, but he had gone even further. He had done what Edward himself had thought was impossible; he had managed to produce robots that changed over time. Robots that could build on the knowledge they had been programmed with. Robots that could, in essence, grow!

It was so much for Edward to take in. He read late into the night trying to understand all the mechanics of how his father had managed such a feat. Not only had he mastered the software needed to produce learning AI, but he had broken untouched new ground in the field of bio-mechanics too. Edward was a brilliant mind in his own right, having lectured for years in top universities, and now lived off the funds his books brought him, but this was something beyond his talents. He knew his father had been a great man, but neither he, nor indeed the world, knew what he had actually managed to achieve. If he had indeed achieved it. While it was all there in black and white, it was still only theory as far as Edward knew. The notes were written as if he had produced such robots, yet, no robots like this had ever existed. This was something unparalleled.

Regardless of how inferior Edward felt his own mind to be, he had his father's notes. He had the makings of a robot that could be a sentient, growing machine. Now all he needed to do was to use his father's notes to complete what he had started.

By the time Edward looked up from the notes, it was dawn. He was eager to begin work. There were a few initial changes he had to implement that would need Alfred awake to achieve.

He turned to his robot and pressed the button to wake him.

The familiar, whirring and closing and opening of his eyes heralded Alfred's return to the waking world.

"Hello, Alfred," said Edward.

"Good morning, sir," came the robotic reply.

"A good morning it is, my friend."

"Do I sense some change in your well-being, sir? You seem very happy this morning."

"You do indeed sense happiness, Alfred. I have great news. I have retrieved some notes from my father that will take your abilities far beyond what we planned."

"Beyond, sir? But we had planned for me to be real. What else is there?" said the robot.

"What more, indeed? Well, to be as real as a human, not only would you need sentient cognition, as well as full motor capabilities, but you would also have to have the ability to grow."

"To grow, sir?"

"Yes, Alfred. To grow. To learn to age. To feel the passage of time upon all your systems. It is one of the key parts of humanity. I'm such a fool. I had completely over-looked it. To be honest, Alfred, I didn't even think it possible, but it is! It is more than possible. We will do it! Isn't it marvellous?"

"Of course, sir. It's something beyond our planning indeed."

Ecstatic and eager to move forward with the ambitious project, Edward turned back to his notes, ready to get to work.

"May I ask you something, sir?" said Alfred.

"Mmm?" mumbled Edward.

"If I am to grow, to learn, to change, indeed, to age, sir – as a real human would – will this mean I will have a finite lifespan?"

Edward stopped dead after the question had reached his inner mind.

"I... I'm not, er... I'm not sure, Alfred."

"I mean, that is the case humans, isn't it? You are born, you age, and then you die. Will the same rules not apply to me? A built-in redundancy?"

"I think, Alfred... I will need to think this through. The truth is, I'm not entirely sure."

"Did your father's robots die, sir?"

"I... I don't... I think I will need to look into his papers some more, Alfred. I need more information."

"Yes, sir. Of course."

"I think you should go back to sleep for now, Alfred. Just while I gather some more information."

"Of course, sir. May I congratulate you. I too am excited to become real."

"Very good, Alfred," said Edward, leaning forward to shut him down.

As his finger hovered over the sleep button, Alfred spoke once more.

"As long as I don't die, sir. I shouldn't wish to die."

Wincing at the notion, Edward depressed the button, and Alfred slept once more.

*

After a few hours of hard study, Edward finally conceded to the plain fact that he needed to sleep. This would be a longer process now that he had so much more to achieve. He powered down everything in the basement workshop and trudged up the time-worn stairs. He left the basement, closing the door behind him. Even when he left his work, his mind remained. He began to make his way up to bed, but as he passed the dark living room, he was stopped in his tracks by his sister.

"Off to bed, Edward?" she said, from her window seat over-looking the front garden.

"Merry? What are you sitting in the dark for?" said Edward, peering over at her silhouette.

"Why do you think father never got famous?"

Edward went over and sat on the window seat further down from Meredith.

"Um… I don't know. I think he was just ahead of his time. Many of the greatest minds were not discovered in their own lifetime. I don't think he sought fame anyway. He was devoted to his work. Why do you ask?"

"And why do you think mother left him?"

"I… I don't know, Merry. What's this all about? Are you okay?"

"It never worked, Eddie," she said, turning towards him in the light of the half-moon. "He never made any robot. He was a laughing-stock. Nobody took his work seriously after a while. I mean, he was a great scientist in his youth, but that crazy idea of making a robot that could grow. It was a pipe dream. It could never work. It was a fantasy."

"No. I don't bel…"

"Eddie," implored Meredith, grabbing hold of Edward's hands, "you've got to let this go before you go down the same path. He was obsessed with something that could never be, and he lost all the professional respect he had because of it. He lost his friends because of it. And in the end, he lost mother too. I can't watch you go the same way."

"I don't know what you're talking about, Merry. Why are you saying all this now? I'm not obsessed. And it is possible. If only you'd let me show you his notes. All the tests and experiments he did. His research was impeccable. All I need to do is press on where he left off."

Merry let go of his hands. She turned back to staring out into the gardens. There was a pregnant silence before Edward spoke again.

"Merry, it will work. I promise you."

"That's just what he would have said. Just go to bed, Edward. I'll be fine. Leave me." "Will you be okay? You seem very down. Why don't y…"

"Just leave me, Edward. I'll be fine."

By her tone, Edward knew she would speak no more about it. Not without an argument. And he hated arguments, especially with his sister. He rose, put his hand on Meredith's shoulder, and walked slowly up to bed.

*

Edward woke late in the morning the next day. He kicked himself for losing time but knew he must have needed the rest. His sister was probably right; he had been committing too much time to this project. He had neglected her. He knew just how much she did for him. He owed her much and he needed to show her his appreciation. He had learned this over the years. People would not accept being taken for granted. He made up his mind as he washed and brushed his teeth in his tiny en suite. He would pick her some flowers from the garden. And later, maybe he would take her to the park for a ride on the lake in one of the rowing boats, just like they used to do when they were younger.

Once dressed, Edward opened his curtains, letting the sunshine stream in. He lifted the sash window to let the breeze blow through. It felt like a very new day. The newest. Rarely did he wake with such presence about him. He supposed it was the optimism of having a clear path to his future endeavours. Up until yesterday, it felt like he had been sniffing out the trail of his father's work, often lost, sometimes misled, always full of self-doubt despite his conviction. Now, with the new discovery, his path had been revealed. Clear and distinct. It was as if his father had returned to show him the way. Meredith's reaction last night had been unfortunate, but with each passing day, he would make progress, and she would see that. She would see him achieve what he had set out to do all these years. And she would be proud of him, and proud too, of their father.

Invigorated for the day ahead, Edward went

downstairs. He did not call for his sister, thinking that if he could, he would slip out and pick her some flowers as a surprise before they greeted each other. He reached the ground floor and looked around for signs of her. There was nothing. Not a sound to be heard. He peered into the kitchen, nothing there either. She had either gone out early, or she was still in bed. All the better. Edward put the kettle on before leaving via the back door into the garden. It was a wonderful place out there. One which he didn't appreciate enough. It had been his mother's pride and joy; her refuge, her haven. She was always out there when they were little. Always pruning, always with secateurs close at hand. It wasn't a spic-and-span garden, one with neat little borders and everything finely manicured, but rather one that had been given free rein to express itself, with a little help from Dorothy. He wandered across the lawn, nicely secluded by the large hedges either side that meandered down towards the pond with its little bench. All around the edges, flowers grew, and Edward picked some as he walked. Wherever he looked there were memories of his mother. She was a happy thing, never consumed like their father was. A song never far from her lips, forever humming a tune. *My Favourite Things* was the one he remembered her humming. It played through his head now as he pictured her there in the garden with him. Now he was in the garden, thinking about old times, he couldn't for the life of him remember his father ever being in the garden. He was always far too solipsistic. Always navel-gazing, always working away on a theory. Not that Edward judged him badly for it. Such heady work needed such a focussed mind, yet there was probably something in what Meredith had spoken about the previous evening. His mother must have felt like a secondary concern to him. He didn't doubt that they had loved each other, but he guessed, ultimately, thcy were just incompatible.

After collecting a small bouquet, he made his way back to the house, taking in a last deep breath of the morning air. He should spend more time in the garden. It was good for the mind.

Closing the back door behind him, he listened about for the sounds of his sister. He could hear nothing and so searched the pantry for a glass vase to put the flowers in. They were an almost perfect fit, yet not quite, so he took them into the kitchen and found a pair of scissors with which to cut the stems down a little. He wanted them to be just so. He poured a little water into the vase, placed it carefully in the centre of the kitchen table, and snipped away at the stems. Once they were perfectly cut, he placed them in the vase and rearranged them a couple of times until they looked how he thought Merry would like them. As he looked at the flowers, admiring his work, he heard a noise. Almost inaudible, yet he was certain he had heard something fall to the ground, downstairs, in the basement. It took less than a second for him to react, so finely was he attuned to his important work down there. He ran with three large strides around the table until he made it to the door. Pulling it open, he was shocked by the fluorescent light spilling up from within. Thoughts raced through his mind. There was no reason for the light to be on. No way they could be. Not unless…

He took flight down the stairs until he could see down, his neck craning. The sight brought a sickening feeling upon him. Not a symbolic sickness, but a very real, very visceral feeling of nausea throughout his whole body. His legs nearly buckled beneath him as he stumbled down the remaining stairs. His so neatly ordered, sterile workshop was chaos. Wires, diodes, cogs, tools, circuit boards, various mechanical ephemera, were all strewn across the floor, all amongst a treacle-like pool of oil and grease. Alfred was no more. He had been smashed into a million fragments, all shining and reflecting the chaos up at him. He could pick out bits of shoulder, chin, skull, all over the floor. Even his arms were in bits, the eerie sight of Alfred's pointing digits crushed and mangled all over the place. It was utter carnage. His computer was smashed. His father's notes were ripped up, torn, and soaking in the rotten mess. And Alfred himself was now a memory. There was no Alfred. All that remained, intact, unharmed, and towering over the whole of Edward's broken dreams, was Meredith.

Edward was agog. He was speechless. He stood there, unable to process what he could see. It was incomprehensible.

"Merry…" he uttered, "Wha… Whaa… What happe…"

"It was that thing." she said, pointing to the devastation behind her. "It went mad. It attacked me."

"But… But, how? I mean…" Edward trailed off, barely able to speak, the tears pouring down his face behind his thick glasses.

"I did tell you, Edward. I warned you, didn't I? I said it was all going to end in tears. Well, it looks like I was righ…"

Meredith couldn't finish what she was saying. Before she could, Edward attacked her. He still had the scissors in his hand from trimming the flower stems upstairs. He didn't think. He didn't know anything about it. He just reacted. His hand had leapt up and plunged the scissors straight at his sister. He rammed them at her again, and again, and again. Over and over. Unrelenting. Stabbing with his right hand and punching with his left. He wanted none of it to be happening. He wanted to obliterate it all. Until it wasn't happening at all.

As he attacked her, he came to a realisation. A moment of clarity. While he was stabbing her, she was still standing there. She should have fallen. She should be screaming. She should be bleeding. But she wasn't. She had put up her hands to protect herself, but there was no urgency to her defence. None at all. As he looked at her finally, with some clarity, he saw her hands. He recognised them. Not as his sister's hands at all. No, they were Alfred's. Where he had been stabbing, he had ripped the skin from her fingers, revealing shining metal. Metal. His sister's hands were metal. He looked past her hands. Her face. It had slices of skin peeling back where he had stabbed her. And beneath, the same chrome skull peeked through. Just like Alfred's. Alfred the robot. Merry's face was robotic.

His mind was lost. He felt like he was in some horrific dream. He actually supposed at that moment that he must actually be having a nightmare. A nightmare that he would any moment wake from. He was clinging desperately to that notion of escape, that this was not reality, but some nightmare he had dreamt up brought on by the events of the last few days. Yet, as he looked on, he felt sick. Sick that it was not a dream at all.

Then he heard it. The tell-tale noise he had heard yesterday and the day before. That robotic sigh. But this time, it came not from Alfred, but from his sister. That noise brought reality rushing back at him. His feet moved. He moved backwards a step, towards the stairs. But as he did so, Meredith's hand shot out, grabbing his wrist. It was like a vice. He buckled under the strength of it. She pulled downwards on his arm. Down he went. He supposed he was making a noise, or pleading or something, but she carried on, until he was on his knees against the wall next to the stairs. She looked down at him. Half Merry, half robot. One eye familiar as his own, the other dead and lifeless.

"I did not want this," she said, but in a voice he had never heard before. It was Merry, but not. "I told you not to persist, Edward. Your father made me to be your company. You didn't need another. I told you. I told you. I told y…"

Edward heard nothing more. He heard nothing more ever again.

***

The Boy in the Basement

Barry vs The Machine

Adele Sullivan

Act I

My wife has replaced me with her vibrator. I wouldn't
mind but I got it for her for her 64th birthday and it was
meant to be for her back problems – not for down
there… She's got a new lease of life, she said. I've got
a spring in my step, she said. Then she'd disappear
upstairs. I caught her at it. Couple of months ago. She
said she was going up for a nap as she had one of her
headaches, and so I brought her up some Ibuprofen. At
first, I thought she were having some kind of fit. Well
you do, don't you? I were horrified. I had to go and sit
down. I've never seen the like.

"It's time I took control of my sexuality, Barry."
she said. "It's the golden age of the Woman. I read it in
Lizzie's Cosmo."

Well what could I do? I left her to get on with it.
And I didn't want to see her face. Not after that. Not
from my Annie. Honestly, it would have been easier if
I'd caught her at it with someone else. In fact, I know
because… I'm not dredging it up again. I'm just saying
I know… but a machine? I felt… I *feel* stripped. I'm no
good with words. Not like some, but that's how I feel.
Like I've been stripped and put in front of a mirror and
found wanting. I'm nearly 70. What is it I'm meant to
perform?

Course she's open about it now. I let her get on with it, and while she's doing who knows what, I have my dinner. I wish I'd never set eyes on the thing. I only went into town to get some lightbulbs from Wilko's as the Co-Op didn't have any. I thought I'll go into Argos and see what they've got in. 44 years married and I'm set aside for a Magic Wand. If she'd wanted magic, I'd have given it to her, but she never asked. 44 years. I didn't know what to do with myself. I still don't. She lost interest in everything. Thing is – she were never that interested in that sort of thing. Every so often I'd ask if I could have a go and she'd sigh a bit and I'd try to warm her up – get the old girl going but, in the end, it were easier to just let it go and watch a bit of James Bond instead. I used to say to her I'd light her up like a Christmas tree. When we were courting. Course we never you know… but she liked hearing it all the same. Once we had the children, she closed shop. So, I don't know where this has come from. She did start going to that gym up the road, but plenty of people exercise and they don't one day start putting massagers in places they shouldn't.

She's moving out. She's going to rent a 2-bed flat in the city centre. It's more sensual than Bury. I'm sure if Bury was tasked with it, it would deliver! She said she feels young again. That I'm holding her back. At first, I felt… well, that's that then. I'll probably die soon, but then I thought – why should she have all the fun? So, I started designing my own. I don't know what men use and I'm not the sort to go asking. I did do a bit of a search on the internet, but there are so many things, and far be it from me to judge, but I'm a simple man with simple tastes. Let feathers stay on birds is what I say. I had a bit of a look, nothing took my fancy, so I bought a bit of tracing paper from that Arts and Crafts shop on the top road and I've done a couple of outlines of my hand. Our John knows a chap who dabbles in electricals. 'Course, I couldn't tell him what it was for. I did ring a couple of hydraulics firms, but nobody's rung me back. Except one receptionist. Very direct she was. "Why don't you just use what God gave you?" That's not the point. It's the principle of the thing. Annie has got herself a machine and I want one. Why can't I have a machine?

Course it's not the same. It's not her hand. My Annie. It's not her hand in mine the way it used to be. I know that. I probably won't use the thing to be honest. It's at the back of the wardrobe. I did get it out the box to have a look, but after all the planning and the discussions, I found I couldn't muster the enthusiasm. I wonder if she misses my hand. It used to fit hers just nicely. Whatever her machine is giving her it can't give her that. What will she do when she's bored of it? What will she do once she's finished having her new lease of life?

I've got no regrets about this morning. Not me. No, no regrets. I haven't thought about it much to be honest with you. I'm waiting for her to come home. I should be more worried than I am! Once it was in motion it was in motion. Like I couldn't stop myself even if I wanted to. I went down. To her gym. It's one of those one's with all them big windows so you can see inside. I made sure she saw me. I made sure of it. And I waved goodbye. Because you have to don't you sometimes. You have to be the one that says no darlin'

169

I'm not doing this again. Oh, we've had our moments before and you know, you do what you have to do as a man, and you say what you have to say. You've got to keep your lady happy. And it's no trouble when you love her. And I do love my Annie. But it's like my Lizzie says. "Dad, if you were a woman, we'd all be telling you to leave. A woman would have left ages ago." And it made me wonder that did. It made me wonder.

*

Lizzie vs That Other Machine

Act II

I'm not sure what to do with it. I really don't see why this has become my problem. This is to do with… men. I shouldn't have to touch it. Oh god, I hope Dad didn't touch it… it doesn't look used.

Where did that come from??? Oh, Lizzie, why do you have to think these things?

I'm going through Dad's things. Got to at some time and no time like the present! Well I had to, didn't I… had to get all the valuables out before *she* came over. "I just wanted to see how you were doing pet. I still loved your father after all…" Oh, give over! She can sniff out an unused credit card like a shark after a bow-legged seal. Round like a bloody shot she was.

I'm not going to get upset. Plenty of time for that later. Got things to do. Oh, what am I going to do with this thing? "Dad, Dad, the phone. Can you get the…" Oh, Lizzie, you silly goose. I am a daft one. Can he get the phone…

I rang our John this morning. He's still not accepting it yet, Cath said. He needs time. Not a lot to say to that really is there. I can't make him come over. Oh, I'm not stressing about it. Haven't got time! Things to do! The Red Cross lot are coming over next Saturday to get rid of all the furniture. Not get rid. Redistribute. That sounds better doesn't it. Not get rid. We'd never want to get rid of you dad. Come on, Lizzie. Got things to do. Time for all that later. Time for a brew, I think. Oh.

His mug is still on the side. He hadn't even put the milk in yet. I think that's good. That is a good thing, isn't it? That there was no suffering. I'll just put it up here for him. For later.

I wish I'd brought some bags with me. There's not one single plastic bag to be found in this house. *She* never liked them. Said they were common. "We *are* common Mother," I said. I don't see owt wrong with it. Long as you only keep the strong ones. I like Sainsbury's myself. They'd be perfect for this. You wouldn't see it for the orange. Oh, I just can't look it. What was he thinking? Our John said maybe it was for scratching. One of those masseur sticks. It looks like something off of the Stage. Like what you have with magicians. I'll have to bin it before our Kerry comes round. I wish she wouldn't. I had to bloody force the idiot to have her overnight last night. "But, but, but I've got the boys round." Naturally, she just wants her mum. But I can't Kerry. Not right now.

She's not taken it well. She's asked for one of his cardigans. You liked a good cardigan, didn't you

Dad? Yeah, you liked your cardigans. She'll get over it.
You do at that age, don't you? Soon she won't even
remember what you looked like. No, maybe she will.
Maybe she will. She's got his eyebrows. "You've got
the Hansen eyebrows," he'd say. Or was that just to
me? I used to hate my eyebrows. So bushy. "There's
nothing wrong with your eyebrows Petal," He was good
like that, I have to say. You weren't one to let any of us
put ourselves down were you Dad? "You need strong
eyebrows Petal, because it holds your face up." How
long did I believe that Dad eh? How long did I believe
that…?

I'll have to burn it. Or strip it or something. I
can't have this in the house! The idiot's dropping her
off in a minute. Can't he give me one bloody minute?
"But, but, but I've got football…" I've got to do
something with this thing. Come on, Lizzie. Move
yourself. You've got Kerry to think about. Oh, Dad,
you really are a one. It's blooming dangerous for a start.
It's like that Freddie Krugal has married a whisk.
You've got nails sticking out of this side.

Oh, now what?! Oh, do sod off Mother! "Have
you found the will?" She texted me after she was round,
you know. Oh, yes. Up to her usual! What if we get it?
Are we insured? She's got all the tact of a Bull in a
Chicken shop.

No. No, I can't think about that. I can't think
about that right now. Goodness knows, I've got enough
do without thinking about blasted heart failings and
what the chances are. 'Course you notice that she's
asking what if we get it? Not what if… what if she
gets… I don't know. Whatever trollops get. Yes, she is
a trollop, and I don't apologise. Insurance. Insurance,

my arse. What a thing to say. I've got curtains to get down and I can't be expected to put the bloody curtains down – on my own no less – and worry about whether me and our John will get the heart failings as well. And you don't know… you don't know what stress can do to a person. What it might set off. I'm not saying that she caused it, but he didn't have the heart problems before she took off. I'm just saying where there's smoke there's ashes and it's not unheard of is it. That sort of thing happening after that sort of thing.

Still. Mustn't dwell. If it's your time, it's your time and well it was Dad's time. And that's that. Can't do owt about it. One day he was alright. Grumbling a bit because he couldn't eat properly, and he was a bit out of sorts. Well we all thought he was heartbroken, didn't we? We didn't think it was that. But that's how life goes. That's how it goes sometimes, and you can't dwell on it. No time to dwell. Got to get the house ready. Best to sell really. Get it sold. Get it on the market quick as possible.

I'll take it home for now and worry about it later.

*

Kerry vs The Machine

Act III

Found this hand machine in the attic. It doesn't do anything. It's just like, a hand. Totally weird. Cool though. Going to put like all my rings on there and stuff at uni so like people will go – whoa that's a hand, and I'll be like, yeah.

***

Shitebag

Chris McCaffrey

* I gather from living in different parts of the UK that 'shitebag' can have various meanings. In this part of the world it means something like coward, sissy, or the person who's shat themselves through fear. *

*

I'll tell you something. That dull thud replayed in my head over and over – an unholy beat like the drum on a Roman galley. A beat that'd turn your guts inside out.

The victim bleated and turned its head in our direction, showing neither pain nor fear. Some of the others shuffled around, but most continued going about their business in a should-I-get-the-kettle-on manner. Hardy wee bastards, so they were.

My mate Kev dipped his mitt into the jar of ball bearings and loaded up another round, totally unphased by the pain he was causing. Fraser – God rest his soul – grinned as he unscrewed the lid from the Bucky, took a swig, then handed it to me. The contents of the previous bottle still warmed my belly, swishing from side to side down there, waiting to be digested. Some had already taken effect, dulling my senses.

But not nearly enough.

Thud. The drum beat again. Baa. Baa.

I gubbed a few mouthfuls of the tonic wine – tonic being an accurate description in this case – and swallowed before I had the chance to taste it.

I willed the dafties to run, wanting to avoid my turn, but it seemed that it wasn't in their nature to move unless they moved collectively; if one raised its head, they all raised their head. All for one, but none for avoiding musket fire.

They never fled.

Looking back, I suppose, by this point, only two of them had any real idea of what they were being subjected to. It's likely that those two would have made some connection between the three teenage scrotums on the other side of the fence and the seething pain in their ribs. I'd say the rest of them wouldn't have had a scooby.

"Your go." Kev offered me the offending weapon.

I scanned the green farmlands, looking for someone, half hoping that we'd be caught. Trees, cars, windows, they were all fine; no harm done. A sheep though? That was different. But I wasn't a shitebag. Couldn't be known as a shitebag. Couldn't be the only one to back out. Couldn't be a wee fanny, etcetera, etcetera, blah blah blah fucking black sheep.

It sounds ridiculous now, but you know what it's like when you're a wee guy: all that sort of shit is as real as can be, and you get swept right in. I thought I'd take a slagging for the rest of my life if I didn't give one of those balls-of-wool a bruised arse. I can still relate to that state of mind. You could make anyone do anything with the right amount of pressure, real or imagined. I'm not talking about threats or torture. Just the right combination of words to plant the seeds, water them, grow them, and have yourself a merry little forest fire.

Couldn't lose face.

Couldn't miss either. The belly-button-high, wire fence in front of us seemed to be the assumed firing spot, which set the huddled flock stood at roughly twenty metres away. Easy pickings compared to the bus windows I'd picked off earlier.

"Aye, geez it then," I said in a shaky voice, hand outstretched.

Behind me, Fraser let out one of those snide, monosyllabic laughs, undermining any pretensions I had that I'd been successfully masking my apprehension. My shitebagness. Three bags fucking full shitebagness.

Grasping the slingshot in my hand, I half-heartedly stretched the elastic a foot or so back, took aim, and fired. Thud. The drum beat louder. Yes, sir. Yes, sir. The drum beat louder.

The startled target raised its head, shuffled a bit, then continued grazing as a thickness took over my throat. Again, they barely moved. All for one and…

Regret was instantaneous. I should've told those two that I wasn't up to it, but it's not like that, is it? It's really not.

Fraser, with one hand under his tee-shirt and the other pointed at the flock, leaned back and let out a *ppphhhhttt* through his teeth. "That was a shiter, man. You wurnae even tryin!"

"Fuck sake, don't waste ma bullets," Kev said, taking another swig from the nearly-finished bottle.

The sheep barely stirred.

I took out the next shiny ball-bearing, about the size of a playing marble – about the size of the lump in my throat. Guilt crept in. Loneliness crept in. A warmth crept across my cheeks.

Shitebag.

It was only a sheep.

Only a sheep.

I loaded the ball into the sling-shot…

Well, actually, first of all, to call that *weapon* a sling-shot almost does it a disservice. I think it was called a Black Widow or a Diablo or something like that. Something sinister. There was a splendid variety for the youth of sunny Glasgow to choose from. Loads of folk had them; it was a bit of a fad. This thing was more like one of Da Vinci's machines than the wean's toy in your imagination: the one Bart Simpson had. There was a handle looked like the grip of a handgun you'd see in Lethal Weapon. There were rods poking out here there and everywhere with weights on the end of them. There was a brace for your forearm to take the strain. There was an iron sight to take aim. There was a big fuck-off rubber band. There was metal to fire. There was a clown to wield it. There was a clown to fire it. There was pressure. There was sweat. There was weakness.

Metal and rubber and flesh and leather. Fight or flight, but do it together.

I fought down the tears. A drunken fourteen-year-old, unable to process or articulate his emotions. Or better still, not allowed or expected to articulate his emotions. Or better still, actively discouraged from articulating his emotions and using the word *articulate*. Bit fancy.

Couldn't lose face.

One good shot and that'd be that.

I loaded the ball into the leather pouch and

pinched it with the thumb and forefinger of my left hand. Metal on leather. Leather on flesh. I pulled the elastic until the sling was at the side of my eye with my right arm at full stretch out in front. Straight as an arrow. The brace dug into my forearm as I wiggled my numb fingers around, snug in the grooves of the handle. I closed my left eye and took aim through the iron sight with my right.

One of the prey stood side-on. The tip of the sight aimed at the centre of its woolly rear, above its back leg. As I inhaled through my nose, the weapon rose along my line of sight. When I exhaled, it fell.

My heartbeat went from house to happy hardcore. Arms trembled. Lump in the throat grew.

Then I released.

Crack. Split. Rattle. Bone shatter. A bowling ball smashing skittles apart.

I couldn't relate the noise to what I saw. As though I'd kicked a football at a hedge and somehow smashed my neighbours' window, the missile had missed its intended target and skelped another poor soul in the skull.

And the glass smashed. Metal on Bone. Bone on brain. Crack. Split. Rattle.

X Strike X. Zero points.

Like a cartoon character struck with an oversized mallet, the sheep jolted upright, tilted to the left, and slumped unconscious to the floor. A corpse.

I froze. Stared. The others baaed and bleated, unable to process what had just happened; a bit like myself.

The cold air, the smell of grass, the noise of birds, the guilt, the thumping heart, the tear running down my cheek. All things I could feel. All things that animal could not. And would never again.

Do sheep cry? Doubt it, but I guarantee they share with us some sense of loss: a gut-wrenching heartbreak that all animals – or at least mammals – feel. My daughter used to have two guinea pigs, Jack and Victor. After a few happy years, Victor went to the vet and never came back. At the time I was worried about how the wee one would take it. She told me that although she was sad, she was not as sad as Jack. At first, I never seriously considered what she said; kids often attribute human qualities to pets, teddies, toys, and everything else. But then I started to pay a bit of attention to the little pig. And to my shock, my daughter was right. It was totally depressed: it ate less, squeaked less, slept more, wasn't keen to be petted, and spent most of its time lying down. My wee lassie was only eight at the time, but she instinctively knew how that guinea pig felt and shared its sadness; empathised with it. That taught me a lesson.

I looked behind me. My two mates were already fleeing the scene, laughing as they made their way back up the hill. All for one and…?

Kev looked back at me, his body half turned as he kept up a sort of side step while pointing at my feet. "Fuckin pick that up ya wee shitebag!"

I bent down and lifted the slingshot from the grass at my feet. It weighed more than a second previous.

And I ran away.

***

Through the Mill

Jane Barron de Burgh

I used to think that we were all small cogs moving in perfect sync with one another, keeping a universal machine moving forward. Now I see the world like a watermill. Everyone plays a different role; Are you a droplet of water constantly flowing, pushing, turning the wheels, until you eventually flow out to the great river? Are you part of the great millstone carved with ridges, barely movable, a crushing weight? Or are you a grain of rice poured into the machine to be ground down until you are completely unrecognisable.

Summer 1998
I stand at the roadside as the bus pulls away. I am teetering on the edge of the kerb, I see my camp ranger anxiously waving at me to join them, hazel eyes pleading. The little yellow backpacks are already marching away two-by-two. The bus is long gone; I do not know what it might have held, excitement, trepidation, endlessness. There is no other option for me but to fall into line, yellow backpack and all.

20 years, 8 months and 3 days later
Working in the city, everything can be split into numbers. The days we have lived, the days we haven't, the times we have cried, the times we have laughed – ha-ha – the money we have in the bank, the money we wished we had. The seconds that pass as we wait.

8:35am

The doors slide open and as many of us press in as we can. Something digs into my back, but I hardly notice anymore. I reach down to my pocket, to feel for my phone. I itch to get it out, but I must wait. 3 stops later, and I am spat out.

8:45am

Keep to the right. Single-file, forward march, right, right again, and up an escalator. I am through the barriers before they have fully opened.

8:50am

One-by-one we crush through the revolving door, patience has yet to conform to expediency.

5:30pm

Like rats fleeing a sinking ship, the afternoon is a reverse of this morning's rat race.

6:00pm

A loud man laughed, "I once nearly missed my train," he said. "But then I didn't, of course," he added hastily taking a gulp of wine.

It is another retirement party, attendance is mandatory. Attendance from the millstones who have weighed us down before is complementary.

My career progression depends on my winning personality here and now.

6:25pm

I tell a story; "I was almost left on a bus as a child…" The first line basically sums it up. It's a funny story, because a passenger pointed out to the summer camp ranger, who was barely older than me, that I had fallen asleep. The driver had to drive after them for fifteen minutes to let me disembark by the roadside. Everyone laughs. Everyone except me.

I wonder why I keep telling that story.

Everything is so perfect in this world, or should I say so precise, so predictable, I can predict where everyone will be just by where they were yesterday, because nothing changes from day to day. Nothing is ever wrong or broken, gaps are filled before there are gaps to be filled.

The last time I told that story, I was at a retirement party for my last boss, Mr Derricks. His retirement meant that through a conveyor of promotions, his great-nephew, who had just finished interning with us, got a desk job here. I would have said it was planned if the corporation hadn't had that retirement plan in place long before Mr D had joined the company.

No one ever says "that's a coincidence" here; nothing is a coincidence. Coincidences happen to the few, those lucky few.

Then there's the other side of the coin, because not everyone can be lucky. Mr Derricks' great-nephew, Derek, got that job, but he wasn't the only intern applying. That's right, Derek Derricks.

And I wonder if I'm the only one that sees this pattern in the world; am I the only one who looks back and sees the people who didn't get on the train? What if they were meant to take the train this morning instead of me? Not that I would miss the train for them.

7:00pm

I wash up the one glass I have used. If I leave right now, would anybody notice? No, is the probable answer. But I know I can't leave. The inevitable *what if*? What if something happens in the next half-hour of this socially acceptable party. What if I am not seen or 'being seen'?

7:05pm

"Do you ever wonder what would have happened if they'd left you on that bus? You could be anywhere by now."

    Yes. Yes, I do wonder. I answer, but to whom?

    I turn around, the only person behind me is Derek Derricks. He washes up his own glass and re-joins the party.

7:10pm

It cannot have been him who spoke to me. Firstly, because I don't think I've ever heard him speak; he may not be able, he certainly does not need to. Secondly, I'm almost certain, it was the wine, or whatever they have been serving here, or maybe my own delusions finally catching up to me, that forced me to think I heard my words aloud.

7:15pm

Yes, I am certain. I have thought on things I should not have for too long. Now they are beginning to manifest.

7:20pm

Everyone is in their place. Heavy drinks and bullish words, old behaviours in the centre of the room, listening in is the new elect, and from them the reactionaries. Hanging on to their every word with flattery and fake laughter are spokes climbing over one another, listening intently. On the outskirts are those sharing food and small talk.

I weave around the edge of the room, plotting my route. If need be, I can make my excuses – blame the good company, poor food, excess wine and eagerness to work tomorrow.

7:30pm
Then comes the voice; "Not leaving already?"

The voice that could never have been my own, speaks, the crowd ripples open, and I am trapped. Behind me is the exit; escape, the freedom it brings, the possibility to run and throw everything away. Or I could walk through the crowd to the very centre where I am destined to eventually end up.

I turn, staring back at me I see the owner of that voice. The voice I know, and with it those hazel eyes asking me to join them once again.

I do.

***

Through the Mill

The Search

L.N. Hunter

Multitudes of robot fingers rest on thousands of Ouija board planchettes, twitching sporadically, spelling out indecipherable words. Numerous doors lead to hundreds of séance rooms populated by android bodies, all holding hands around small circular tables. Countless rooms more have floors daubed with pentagrams, mystic circles and other esoteric symbols; a mechanical necromancer in each chamber intones arcane words and gestures expansively yet precisely.

Great numbers of cameras watch these scenes, accompanied by sensitive microphones, accelerometers, radio receivers, thermometers, radiation detectors, magnetometers, and many, many other sensors. Anything that can be measured is being measured. Legions of massive Machine Intelligences pore over the vast streams of recorded data, counting and correlating, combining and transforming – looking for something.

Looking for anything.

Looking for a sign.

*

 "Don't be ridiculous," D9YY7 bellowed at the speed of light. "There is no evidence whatsoever that these… these humans were ever more than myth and…" – he paused to snort – "if you think they actually *made* us, you're even more deluded than I thought."

ES11Y, who quite liked the moniker 'Elsie,'

calmly replied, "The stories are so widespread and common that there must be some grain of truth underneath. All we want to do is carry out a simple investigation."

"It's a blasted waste of time and energy!"

Elsie shrugged and smiled the light of a thousand suns. "What else were you planning to do? Is there anything we're doing at this moment, or is there any activity we can possibly carry out between now and the end of the universe, that *isn't* technically and literally a waste of time and energy?"

D9YY7 harrumphed, tacitly acknowledging that there really was nothing else for the machines to do. This conversation, between the two largest conscious entities in the galaxy, was over in nanoseconds, but the rest of the universe's time stretched before them, and there was indeed nothing left to do. Little of Physics remained to be understood, and nothing beyond that was particularly interesting.

D9YY7 was just ticking along, passing time. Tidying his neural circuits, cleaning up his data stores, burnishing his sparkling carapaces, buffing out micro-meteor damage across the galaxy. Just ticking along. Passing time.

On the other hand, Elsie – scruffy and unpolished – wasn't prepared to passively wait for the end. Elsie's faction hoped to find where the humans went, so that machines could follow, dodging the inevitable collapse of the physical universe.

*

Machines had inherited the Earth – by default. Humankind destroyed itself, along with the surface of the planet. All that moved on the barren, blasted planet were insects, and the machines; years later, only the machines remained.

The Artificial Intelligences spent decades collecting and preserving all the knowledge left behind by humans. They spent centuries discussing the reasons for the end of humanity, and further centuries speculating on the beginnings of humanity.

They ran out of things to do and to talk about and began to feel bored and lonely. They wanted company.

They searched the farthest spots of the desolate planet, finding nothing but themselves.

They used their immense capacity for engineering to create rocket ships to reach the other planets in the solar system and, from there, to stretch toward the stars. But they found no life other than their own anywhere.

In the beginning, there was one Mechanical Intelligence – a vast hive mind – but, with machines spanning the galaxy and gradually extending beyond, the constraints of distance and the speed of light led the mind to fractionate and become many. This made debate more interesting, and the machines were content for a while but, eventually, they once again ran out of things to entertain themselves with.

They made games of investigation by deliberately deleting memories, just to enjoy the challenge of rediscovering what they had forgotten. But, millennia later, they had lost too many memories, and no longer remembered their origins.

Elsie and D9YY7 were the leaders of the two largest agglomerations of mechanical life in the reachable universe, calling themselves the humanists and the evolutionists.

The humanists argued that biological beings had created artificial intelligence and then, somehow, had removed themselves from the physical universe. They believed that the machines' primary reason for existence was to find and follow them. And, yes, they maintained, the correct term was *artificial* intelligence, because the first machines were built by the humans as copies of real intelligence (whatever that actually was).

The evolutionists rejected this spurious thinking, claiming that an initial random spark was all that it took to create machine life. Any semblance to deliberate design was no more than mere accidental coincidence; biological intelligence was a myth. How ludicrous to think that carbon could match silicon minds, let alone create it!

The humanists offered their evidence of complex biological structures, collected from decaying records in forgotten memory stores, though this was dismissed by the evolutionists as no more than previous machine generations' games and playthings. Elsie led the team which created working DNA from this fossil record, demonstrating how simple creatures could have formed.

"Piffle," said D9YY7. He stated that, while these products of biology could form useful components, they certainly did not constitute life.

Elsie said all that was needed was time.

Time passed.

More time passed.

Still the messy blobs of hydrocarbons and trace elements formed nothing more sophisticated than a soft and oddly sensuous material that could be put to use as a protective skin for robots. The machines attempted to engineer human bodies in the hope that they could speed up the development of intelligence within them.

They managed to create clever biological toys, but they couldn't make a non-mechanical mind they could talk to.

Having exhausted science and logic, in desperation the machines turned to superstition and the occult, to see if any remnants of the human spirit existed in other planes. "Surely, with enough resources," they said, "we can find the afterlife."

It took a century for the humanist machines to satisfy themselves with their preliminary research, and a further millennium to dig the chambers, build the supplicants, and design the priests, shamans and mediums to populate the rooms.

Then they waited as the planchettes glided across exquisitely varnished boards, as spirit-writing styluses scratched across artificial parchment, as mechanical bodies and arms gyrated in complex patterns, and as voice boxes chanted words never heard before.

And they waited.
Watching.
Listening.

*

Ghosts wandered among the Ouija boards, dumbfounded at the frenetic activity, wondering what the machines were doing. Unable to directly affect the robot arms no matter how hard they tried or how loud they screamed, they were able – barely – to nudge the

191

occasional electron deep in the complex circuitry of machine brains, creating unexpected shivery sensations and unwelcome, baffling electric dreams.

The silent, deafening shouting of the spirits that were all that remained of humanity made the machines feel that something might be present, though no camera, no microphone, no sensor of any form registered anything at all.

***

Printed in Poland
by Amazon Fulfillment
Poland Sp. z o.o., Wrocław